LAST NIGHT IN MONTREAL

Emily St. John Mandel was born in Canada. She is the author
of the novels *Last Night in Montreal*, *The Singer's Gun*,
The Lola Quartet and *Station Eleven*. She lives
with her husband in New York City.

LAST NIGHT
IN
MONTREAL

EMILY ST. JOHN MANDEL

PICADOR

First published 2009 by Unbridled Books

First published in the UK in paperback 2015 by Picador
an imprint of Pan Macmillan, a division of Macmillan Publishers Limited
Pan Macmillan, 20 New Wharf Road, London N1 9RR
Basingstoke and Oxford
Associated companies throughout the world
www.panmacmillan.com

ISBN 978-1-4472-8002-6

1 3 5 7 9 8 6 4 2

A CIP catalogue record for this book is available from the British Library.

Typeset by Ellipsis Digital Limited, Glasgow
Printed and bound by CPI Group (UK) Ltd, Croydon, CR0 4YY

To Kevin

PART ONE

1

No one stays forever. On the morning of her disappearance Lilia woke early, and lay still for a moment in the bed. It was the last day of October. She slept naked.

Eli was up already, and working on his thesis proposal. While he was typing up the previous day's research notes he heard the sounds of awakening, the rustling of the duvet, her bare footsteps on the hardwood floor, and she kissed the top of his head very lightly en route to the bathroom—he made an agreeable humming noise but didn't look up—and the shower started on the other side of the almost-closed door. Steam and the scent of apricot shampoo escaped around the edges. She stayed in the shower for forty-five minutes, but this wasn't unusual. The day was still unremarkable. Eli glanced up briefly when she emerged from the bathroom. Lilia, naked: pale skin wrapped in a soft white towel, short dark hair wet on her forehead, and she smiled when he met her eyes.

"Good morning," he said. Smiling back at her. "How did you sleep?" He was already typing again.

She kissed his hair again instead of answering, and left a trail of wet footprints all the way back to the bedroom. He heard her towel fall softly to the bedroom floor and he wanted to go and make love to her just then, but he was immersed so deeply in the work that morning, *accomplishing* things, and he didn't want to break the spell. He heard a dresser drawer slide shut in the bedroom.

She came out dressed all in black, as she almost always did, and carrying the three pieces of a plate that had fallen off the bed the night before. The plate was a light shade of blue, and sticky with pomegranate juice. He heard her dropping it into the kitchen garbage can before she wandered past him into the living room. She stood in front of his sofa, running her fingers through her hair to test for dampness, her expression a little blank when he glanced up at her, and it seemed to him later that she'd been considering something, perhaps making up her mind. But then, he played the morning back so many times that the tape was ruined—later it seemed possible that she'd simply been thinking about the weather, and later still he was even willing to consider the possibility that she hadn't stood in front of the sofa at all—had merely paused there, perhaps, for an instant that the stretched-out reel extended into a moment, a scene, and finally a major plot point.

Later he was certain that the first few playbacks of that last morning were reasonably accurate, but after a few too many nights of lying awake and considering things, the quality began to erode. In retrospect the sequence of events is a little hazy, images running into each other and becoming slightly confused: she's across the room, she's kissing him for a third time—and why doesn't he look up and kiss her? Her last kiss lands on his head—and putting on her shoes; does she kiss him before she puts on her shoes, or afterward? He can't swear to it one way or the other. Later on he examined his memory for signs until every detail seemed ominous, but eventually he had to conclude that there was nothing strange about her that day. It was a morning like any other, exquisitely ordinary in every respect.

"I'm going for the paper," she said. The door closed behind her. He heard her clattering footsteps on the stairs.

HE WAS HUNTING just then, deep in the research, hot on the trail of something obscure, tracking a rare butterfly-like quotation as it fluttered through thickets of dense tropical paragraphs. The chase seemed to require the utmost concentration; still, he couldn't help but think later on that if he'd only glanced up from the work, he might've seen something: a look in her eyes, a foreshadowing of doom, perhaps a train ticket in her hand or the words *I'm Leaving You Forever* stitched on the front of her coat. Something did seem slightly amiss, but he was lost in the excitement of butterfly hunting and ignored it, until later, too late, when somewhere between Andean loanwords and the lost languages of ancient California he happened to glance at the clock. It was afternoon. He was hungry. It had been four and a half hours since she'd gone for the paper, and her watery footprints had evaporated from the floor, and he realized what it was. For the first time he could remember, she hadn't asked if he wanted a coffee from the deli.

He told himself to stay calm, and realized in the telling that he'd been waiting for this moment. He told himself that she'd just been distracted by a bookstore. It was entirely possible. Alternatively, she liked trains: at this moment she could be halfway back from Coney Island, taking pictures of passengers, unaware of what time it was. With this in mind, he returned reluctantly to the work; a particular sentence had gotten all coiled up on him while he was trying to express something subtle and difficult, and he spent an uneasy half-hour trying to untangle the wiring and making a valiant effort not to dwell on her increasingly gaping absence, while several academic points he was trying to clarify got bored and wandered off into the middle distance. It took some time to coax them back into focus, once the sentence had been mangled beyond all recognition and the final destination of the paragraph worked out. But by the time the paragraph arrived at the station it was five o'clock, she'd left to get the paper before noon, and it no longer seemed unreasonable to think that something had gone horribly wrong.

He rose from the desk, conceding defeat, and began to check the apartment. In the bathroom nothing was different. Her comb was where it had always lived, on the haphazard shelf between the toilet and the sink. Her toothbrush was where she'd left it, beside a silver pair of tweezers on the windowsill. The living area was unchanged. Her towel was lying damply on the bedroom floor. She'd taken her purse, as she always did. But then he glanced at the wall in the bedroom, and his life broke neatly into two parts.

She had a photograph from her childhood, the only photograph of herself that she seemed to own. It was a Polaroid, faded to a milky pallor with sunlight and time: a small girl sits on a stool at a diner counter. A bottle of ketchup is partially obscured by her arm. The waitress, who has a mass of blond curls and pouty lips, leans in close across the countertop. The photographer is the girl's father. They've stopped at a restaurant somewhere in the middle of the continent, having been travelling for some time. A sheen on the waitress's face hints at the immense heat of the afternoon. Lilia said she couldn't remember which state they were in, but she did remember that it was her twelfth birthday. The picture had been above his bed since the night she'd moved in with him, her one mark on the apartment, thumbtacked above the headboard. But when he looked up that afternoon it had been removed, the thumbtack neatly reinserted into the wall.

Eli knelt on the floor, and took several deep breaths before he could bring himself to lift an edge of the duvet. Her suitcase was gone from under the bed.

Later he was out on the street, walking quickly, but he couldn't remember how he'd ended up there or how much time had passed since he'd left the apartment. His keys were in his pocket, and he clutched them painfully in the palm of his hand. He was breathing too quickly. He was walking fast through Brooklyn, far too late, circling desperately through the neighbourhood in wider and wider spirals, every bookstore, every café, every bodega that he thought might conceivably attract her. The traffic was too loud. The sun was too bright. The streets were haunted with a terrible conspiracy of normalcy, bookstores and cafés and bodegas and clothing stores all carrying on the charade of normal existence, as if a girl hadn't just walked off the stage and plummeted into the chasm of the orchestra pit.

He was well aware that he was too late by hours. Still, he took the subway to Pennsylvania Station and stood there for a while anyway, overexposed in the grey atrium light, more out of a sense of ceremony than with any actual hope: he wanted at least to see her off, even if it had been four or five hours since the departure of her train. He stood still in an endless parade of travellers passing quickly, everyone pulling suitcases, meeting relatives, buying water and tickets and paperbacks for the journey, running late. Penn Station's ever-present soldiers eyed him disinterestedly from under their berets, hands casual on the barrels of their M-16s.

That night there was a knock on his door, and he was on his feet in an instant, throwing it open, thinking perhaps . . . "Trick or Treat!" said an accompanying mother brightly. She looked at him, started to repeat herself, quickly ushered her charges on to a more promising doorstep. The whole encounter lasted less than a moment ("Come on, kids, I don't think this nice man has any candy for us . . ."), but it remained seared into his memory nonetheless. Afterward, when the thought of Lilia leaving seeped through him like a chill, he never could shake the image of that hopeful line of trick-or-treaters (from left to right: vampire, ladybug, vampire, ghost) like a mirage on his doorstep, no one older than five, and the smallest one (the vampire on the left) sucking on a yellow lollipop. He recognized her as the little girl from the fourth floor who sometimes threw temper tantrums on the sidewalk. She was three and a half years old, give or take, and she smiled very stickily at him just before he closed the door.

Lilia's childhood memories took place mostly in parks and public libraries and motel rooms, and in a seemingly endless series of cars. Mirage: she used to see water in the desert. In the heat of the day it pooled on the highway, and the horizon broke into shards of white. There was a map folded on the dashboard, but it was fading steadily under the barrage of light. Lilia was supposed to be the navigator but entire states were dissolving into pinkish sepia, the lines of highways fading to grey. The names of certain cities were indistinct now along the fold, and all the borders were vanishing. Her seat-belt buckle was searing to the touch. The dashboard clock marked slow-motion time. A mile behind her on the desert highway, a detective was following in a battered blue car.

Her father drove in silence, every so often blotting sweat from his face with a handkerchief. This fever-dream place awash in light, in mirages, the sky white with heat along the horizon on every side, cars mirrored in phantom water on the highway ahead. She found later that most of her childhood memories had a hallucinatory quality, as a result of travelling some distance too far and driving through the desert a few times too often and changing her name so frequently that she sometimes forgot what it was, but her memories of the first year or two of travel were the least precise. Later she could never remember why they had started driving away from everything, and at first her father was rendered in the broadest possible strokes: the hand passing her a Styrofoam cup of hot chocolate in the gas station parking lot, the voice soothing her in a motel room as he cut off all her hair and dyed it, but mostly as a silhouette in the driver's seat, an impression, a voice. He knew the words to half the songs on the radio, and he said things that always made her laugh. He'd tell her anything about everything, except Before. He said it wasn't really that important. He said they had to live in the present. Before was shorthand for the time before he started driving away with her, Before was a front lawn somewhere far to the north. More specifically, Before was her mother.

Lilia's mother was asleep the night her daughter vanished. She didn't hear the sound that woke Lilia up that night, the staccato of ice hitting the windowpane from outside. Lilia remembered that night the way dreams are remembered. It began with a sharp clear sound that pulled her out of sleep. She sat up in the darkness, and the sound came again. She opened the curtains but the glass was foggy, so she opened the window and let in the night. Her father was standing below on the lawn. He waved and held a finger to his lips. She picked up her knitted wool rabbit from the floor and walked down the stairs as quietly as possible, the banister at shoulder height (she was only seven), and her mother was sleeping when she closed the front door behind her.

Fifteen years later in another country Lilia pressed her forehead against a windowpane in Eli's apartment, looking out at an uncharted landscape of Brooklyn rooftops in the rain, and came to a somewhat unsettling conclusion: she'd been disappearing for so long that she didn't know how to stay.

The problem, Eli used to think before he met her, was that he'd never suffered, except insofar as everyone does: the stalled trains, the alarm clocks that don't ring when they're supposed to, the agony of being surrounded by other people who all give the impression of being way more productive and considerably more talented than you are, wet socks in the winter, being alone in any season, the chronic condition of being misunderstood, zippers that break at awkward moments, being unheard and then having to repeat yourself embarrassingly in front of girls you're trying to impress, trying to impress girls and failing, girls who can be seduced but remain unimpressible, girls who can't be seduced and/or turn out to have boyfriends in the morning, girls, being alone, paper grocery bags with falling-out bottoms, waiting in line at the post office for a half-hour and then being snapped at because you don't have the right customs declaration forms to send the birthday gift to your perpetually travelling brother, waiting in line anywhere, phone calls from a disapproving mother who doesn't understand, the crowd of overeducated friends who understand too much and can't resist bringing up long-dead philosophers and/or quantum physics over an otherwise perfectly civilized morning coffee, girls, an overall lack of direction and meaning as evidenced in your inability to either come up with an acceptable topic for your thesis and then write the thesis or heroically give up the whole thing completely and go do something completely different with your life, stepping in things on the sidewalk, lost buttons, most kinds of rain, standing in line at the grocery store behind the lady who just knows there's a coupon in here somewhere, girls, and the sense that all of this adds up to a life that's ultimately pretty shallow and doesn't really mean that much, particularly in comparison to the older brother saving children in Africa. The situation wasn't helped by the mind-numbing job. Eli was paid a reasonable salary to stand in an empty art gallery five days a week, surrounded by art that he found incomprehensible, and there had been a time when he'd considered himself lucky to have found a job like that, involving standing instead of doing, but lately the state of standing still instead of doing things had begun to seem symptomatic to him.

"There's this artist in Asia," Eli said. "I know how to pronounce his name, but I won't. Call him Q. What Q does is he strips down to his underwear, then he coats himself with honey and fish oil, and then he goes and sits next to a latrine in this rural village in China, and so of course then he gets covered in flies because he's hanging out next to the latrine covered in all this honey and fish oil, and so he's sitting there, all covered in flies and all greasy and stoic-looking, and a photographer takes pictures of him, and this is the thing . . ." He realized that he was speaking too loudly and took a quick sip of water to calm himself. "The thing that gets me," he continued in a quieter voice, "is that the pictures then sell for up to eighteen thousand apiece. *Eighteen thousand dollars.* For a photograph of a guy with a hundred or so flies on his skin. All he's doing is sitting there in a G-string, with flies, staring off into space, and he's considered an artist. It kills me."

"Okay," said Geneviève, "he's considered an artist. And? Why would that bother you?" She was sitting across from him at the café table with an incredulous look on her face. He had been lingering at the Third Cup Café with Geneviève and Thomas for years now, but lately he'd been finding it increasingly difficult to talk to them.

"It's the word, I guess." He was silent for a moment. Thomas had set his magazine down on the table. "Yeah, it's the word. *Artist* is the word we use for Chopin, for Handel, for Van Gogh, for Hemingway, these men whose art required a lifetime and unprecedented talent and blood and sweat, these men whose art eventually rendered them dead or insane or alcoholic or all of the above, and we use this same word, *artist*, for a guy who smears honey on his skin and then sits around till some flies show up and then gets his picture taken and makes eighteen thousand dollars for his efforts. If he were mentally ill and did the same thing, you'd lock him up. But because he issues a statement saying that sitting there covered in flies is an act of, of subversion against the, I don't know, some kind of political statement against Chinese communism or Western capitalism or whatever, you call him an *artist*. And they're all like that. Every single so-called artist at this so-called gallery I get paid to stand around in. There's this other guy who dances naked around his tripod with the camera on a timer, and it's supposed to represent, I don't know, his Nigerian heritage or his *joie de vif,* and . . ."

"*Joie de vivre,*" said Geneviève.

"Whatever." He used a coffee-stained napkin to blot sweat from his forehead. "He's just a blurred naked guy."

"Maybe you just don't *get* it," said Geneviève helpfully.

"Jesus—" said Thomas, but Eli cut him off.

"No, she's right. I don't get it. I work in a gallery, I'm supposed to sell this shit, which I consider the work of frauds, I actually *do* sell this shit, which clearly makes *me* a fraud, and I don't get it. I don't think it's good enough. I don't believe we should be calling it art."

"Then what *is* art?" Geneviève asked. "Let's get to the bottom of this. It's eleven A.M.; we can have this figured out by lunchtime."

"Look, I'm not saying I know," Eli said. "I'm not saying I'm any better. I just think you have to do more than take your clothes off in front of a camera. I think you have to have some talent, not just a clever conceptual idea. I think you have to actually create something. They're artists because they issue statements saying they're artists, not because of anything they actually do or produce, and that's really where my problem begins. I'm not claiming to know the answer here."

This quieted Geneviève—she only liked arguing with people who were willing to claim that they *did* know the answer, for the sheer pleasure of tackling them. At a loss, she got up and went to the counter for a coffee refill.

"And this is what's been bothering you lately?" Thomas asked while she was gone. "You've been a little off."

"I don't know. It's not just the artists in the gallery. They're only part of it. I got a letter from my brother the other day."

"Zed?"

"He's the only one I have."

"I haven't seen him around in forever. Where is he these days?"

"Africa somewhere. Working at an orphanage. Before that he was building a school in some village in Peru. In between he went hitchhiking in the Middle East. And the thing with those letters is, they come from these places, and you know why?"

"Because he's in those places?"

"No, look, what I *mean* is the letters come from these unbelievable places because one day years ago he decided to travel, so he travels. He doesn't talk about travel. He doesn't theorize about travel. He just buys a ticket and goes," Eli said. He was watching Geneviève returning to the table with her coffee. "All the theorizing we do. We're all talking about doing things, but no one actually *does* anything. No one ever takes the leap."

"What leap?" Geneviève asked. She was considering him over the rim of her coffee mug.

"They never *do* anything. *We* never do anything. I'm not saying I'm exempt from this. I always thought that once the thesis was done I'd be a linguist and write, you know, really groundbreaking stuff in my field, but let's be honest here, I'm never going to finish my thesis. I've been working on my thesis for six years and I am completely, absolutely stalled."

"And the rest of us?" asked Geneviève dangerously. She hadn't painted anything in a while.

Eli realized he was about to step on a land mine, and retreated.

"Sorry. I'm rambling. Ignore me," he said. He drew a long breath. "Look, I'm not naming names here, I'm not saying I *know* anything, it's just hard not to notice that none of us are actually . . . I'm sorry," he said. "I don't know what's wrong with me today. Forget it."

"It's cool," said Thomas warily.

"Why is it bothering you *now*," Geneviève asked unpleasantly, "if you've been a third of the way in for that long?"

"It's my birthday on Thursday. I'll be twenty-seven, and it dawned on me: *twenty-seven*. It's been years since I've been a promising academic, or a promising anything, actually, and I think my school's actually forgotten about me. I always wondered what would happen when I failed to meet my thesis committee's deadline and hand in the finalized proposal, and then when it happened . . . my deadline passed a year ago, and no one contacted me. No one. There was nothing. It's like I've been struck from the school records, or like I don't exist. And then when I think of Zed, *doing* things, I just don't . . . Look," he said, "I don't want to talk about this. I think I'm going to go for the paper."

"You can get it here."

"And then sit in the park for a bit," Eli said, ignoring this, "and then maybe go home and stare at my thesis. Ciao."

Thomas waved. And he did hear Geneviève's whispered *What the hell's wrong with him?* as he walked out of the Third Cup Café into the brilliant sunlight of Bedford Avenue, but he ignored it. He stood on the sidewalk for a moment and decided not to go to the park after all, instead walked slowly in a diagonal line across the deserted intersection and under the blue awning of the Café Matisse. There was a girl who read books there whom he wanted to meet.

HIS THESIS PROPOSAL DEADLINE passed like a signpost through a slow car window, like the last sign before the beginning of a trackless wilderness. For several nervous weeks after the circled date on the calendar, actually several nervous months, he had a falling sensation in his stomach every time the phone rang. It took some time to realize that no one was going to call him. He wasn't about to call them. He ceased any pretense of being just on the verge of completing the document and immersed himself as completely as he could in research.

Eli never felt particularly calm, or that he was moving even remotely in the correct direction. Still, he felt that the research in itself wasn't without merit: in his effort to narrow his thesis topic down to a manageable scope, he'd become somewhat of an expert in the study of absence. Specifically, dead languages, or if not dead, then at least terminally ill. He had spent an enormous amount of time studying small languages on the edge of extinction: the oldest languages of Australia, California, China, Lapland, obscure corners of Arizona and Quebec, fading out for exactly the reasons one might expect—colonization, the proliferation of residential schools and smallpox, the dispersal of native speakers over vast distances, etc. He'd grown used to watching girls' eyes glaze over when he started talking about it; that Lilia actually seemed to find the whole thing fascinating, watching him seriously across a table at the Café Matisse on the day they met, came as a bright and exuberant shock.

The majority of languages, he told her grandly, will disappear. Since she still seemed interested, Eli flashed his favourite statistics across the table like a Rolex: of the six thousand languages currently spoken on this earth, 90 percent are endangered and half will be gone by the end of the next century. An optimistic few hope to save a handful of them; most linguists hope for nothing more than a chance to document a fraction of the loss. His work was part reconstruction, part thesis, part requiem, he told her. She listened quietly, apparently rapt, and asked intelligent questions just when he thought her interest couldn't possibly be sincere. She said lightly that she was used to much more localized vanishing acts: individual people, motel rooms, cars. She wasn't used to disappearance on a larger scale. Imagine, he said, losing half the words on earth. Although what he was actually trying to imagine just then, as he said that, was what it might be like to kiss her neck. She nodded and watched him across the tabletop.

Three thousand languages, destined to vanish. He'd become obsessed with the untranslatable: his idea, and somewhere in this idea was his thesis if he could only find a way to narrow the focus to one or two languages instead of all of them at once, was that every language on earth contains at least one crucial concept that cannot be translated. Not just a word but an idea, like the French *déjà vu*: perfect and crystalline in its native language, otherwise explainable only by entire clumsy foreign paragraphs or not at all. In Yupik, a language spoken by the Inuit along the Bering Sea, there is *Ellam Yua*: a kind of spiritual debt to the natural world, or a way of moving through that world with some measure of generosity, of grace, or a way of living that acknowledges the soul of another human being, or the soul of a rock or of a piece of driftwood; sometimes translated as *soul*, or as *God*, but meaning neither. In a Mayan language, K'iche, there is the *Nawal*: one's spiritual essence but separate from the self; one's other, not exactly an alter ego or merely an avatar but a protective spirit that cannot be summoned.

And if you accept this, he told her, this premise that every language holds something that exists in no other tongue, an entity far outweighing the sum of its words, then the loss takes on a staggering weight. It isn't so much a question of losing three thousand words for everything. There *aren't* three thousand words for everything; the speakers of Yupik have no reason to describe tigers in the High Arctic; the speakers of the jungle languages need no words for the northern lights. It isn't even so much about the words. His belief was that these are not just languages we lose in the gloaming, not just three thousand sets of every word, but three thousand ways of existing on this earth.

"I'm sorry," he said finally. "I didn't mean to get so pedantic about it."

"It's all right. It's interesting," she said.

She had been listening for a very long time. They'd met early in the afternoon, and it was almost evening now. It had been weeks since he'd first noticed her here, sitting quietly in the Café Matisse when he walked by the window or came in for a coffee. She came here often, and when they were here at the same time he liked to try to sit as nearby as possible. On this particular day, when he'd left Thomas and Geneviève at the Third Cup Café across the intersection, there were no empty tables when he'd wandered in—thank you, God—and in a catastrophe of blind courage he'd walked across to her table, insinuated himself into the opposite seat, and introduced himself. By some small miracle she'd smiled back and said her name instead of telling him to leave her alone and wait for his own goddamn table, and that had been six or seven hours ago. The café was quiet now, and the morning waitress had left for the day. The afternoon waitress was leaning on the countertop, staring out at the uneventful street.

"But what about you?" he asked. "You know I like dead languages, but what do you like?"

"Live languages," Lilia said. "Reading, taking photographs, a few other things. Do you work in the neighbourhood?"

"Yeah, a few blocks from here. I stand in an art gallery staring at the wall five days a week. You?"

"The wall? Not the paintings?"

"There aren't that many paintings there—actually, there aren't *any*—I don't want to talk about my job," he said. "I don't like my job very much, to be perfectly honest. What do *you* do for a living?"

"I wash dishes. Do you like to travel? I went to New Mexico recently; have you been?"

"Several times. And what's interesting," he said, "is that we've been talking for hours now, and I hardly know anything about you. Where are you from?"

She smiled. "This will sound very strange to you," she said, "but I've lived in so many places that I'm not entirely sure."

"I see. Well. How long have you lived in New York?"

"About six weeks," she said.

"And where were you just before that?"

"You mean where was I living when I boarded a train to New York?"

"Exactly. Yes. You arrived here from somewhere."

"From Chicago," she said.

He felt that he was finally getting somewhere. "You lived there for a while?"

"Not really. A few months."

"Before that?"

"St. Louis."

"Before that?"

"Minneapolis. St. Paul. Indianapolis. Denver. Some other places in the Midwest, New Orleans, Savannah, Miami. A few cities in California. Portland."

"Is there anywhere you *haven't* lived?"

"Sometimes I think there isn't."

"You're a traveller."

"Yes. I try to be as upfront about it as possible now," she said.

He wasn't sure what she meant but let it pass. "You said you liked live languages," he said.

"I like translating things."

"What do you translate?"

"Random things that I come across. Newspaper articles. Books. It's just something I like doing."

Four and a half languages not including English, she said, when pressed for more details. Español, Italiano, Deutsch, Français. Her Russian, she admitted, was shaky at best.

"I envy you. I don't speak any living languages except English. What else do you like?"

"I like Greek mythology," she said. "I like that Matisse print over the bar. It's the reason why I come here, actually." She gestured at the opposite wall, and he twisted around to look. *The Flight of Icarus,* 1947: one of Matisse's final works, from the time when he'd subsided from paint into paper cut-outs and was moving closer and closer to the end of the line, unable to walk, his body slipping away from him. Icarus is a black silhouette falling through blue, his arms still outstretched with the memory of wings, bright starbursts exploding yellow around him in the deep blue air. He's wingless, and already close above the surface of the water: Matisse would be dead in seven years. Icarus, plummeting fast into the Aegean Sea, and there's a red spot on him, a symbol, to mark the last few heartbeats held in his chest.

"I like mythology too. When did you get interested in Greek legends?"

"Two days after I turned sixteen."

"That's very specific. You got a book for your birthday?"

"No, someone I knew was talking about the story, so I read it as soon as I could. I don't really know Matisse, but I like that print. I like the story," she said. "I think it's the saddest of all the Greek legends." She blinked, and when she spoke again she sounded tired. "What time is it?"

"Probably eight o'clock or so. May I walk you home?"

"Yes," she said.

HER HOME was a rented room with a window that looked out on an airshaft, a brick wall three feet from the glass. Night fell at one-thirty in the afternoon. The times when he came to her in that room he had the feeling of stepping into a cave, or stepping outside time. She slept on a mattress on the floor. A suitcase, opened against the wall, held a jumble of clothes and a battered manila envelope. She had a Polaroid from her childhood pinned neatly to a wall: Lilia in a diner, twelve years old in the summertime in a far-off Southern state, leaning over the countertop with the waitress.

Lilia: she had ink stains on her fingers, and the most beautiful eyes. She wore a silver chain necklace but wouldn't say where it was from. She was obsessed by the topography of language: she followed the maps of alphabets over obscure terrains, parted the shifting gauze curtains between *window, fenêtre, finestra, fenster* and peered outward, wrote out long charts of words and brought home books in five languages. She maintained a secretive, passionate life of study. She was without precedent. Eli had dedicated his life before her to not being alone, he had surrounded himself with other people for as long as he could remember, but he had never known anyone remotely like her.

She had a mind like a switchblade. She sometimes stayed up all night. She worked four or five nights a week washing dishes at a vast Thai restaurant near the river, where Manhattan shone across the dark water at night. She returned from the restaurant at midnight with an aura of dish soap and steam, peanut oil, kitchen grime, her face shiny with exertion and her eyes too bright. She stayed up reading till morning, her lips moving as she struggled with the Cyrillic alphabet.

Her hair was dark and cut unevenly, in a way that he found secretly thrilling. He knew that when it got too long she cut it herself, fast and carelessly, not necessarily in the presence of a mirror. The effect was rough but she was pretty enough to pull it off. She had scars on her arms, a faint and complicated pattern of lines suggesting a long-ago accident involving a great deal of broken glass, visible only under certain lights; she never talked about them, and he could somehow never bring himself to ask. She had four or five unevenly spaced freckles on her nose, like Lolita. She gave the impression of harbouring enormous secrets. She had been travelling alone from city to city, in his understanding, since she was no older than sixteen or seventeen years old. She alluded occasionally to her father in New Mexico and she talked to him on the phone sometimes. Her father had a girlfriend, and they had two small children together, but Eli was never sure if there was anyone else. The existence of a mother, for example, was far from clear. When he asked, she said she'd never known her mother and went quiet.

She moved in with him at the midpoint: three months after he walked her home from the Café Matisse and three months before she disappeared. Cohabitation held certain surprises. She had a specific way of living that seemed to him at once erratic and ritualistic and frequently caused him to wonder about her sanity—a faint unease came over him while sitting beside the bathtub, for example, chatting and watching her shave her legs, change razor blades, and then shave her legs again. She would pause occasionally to sip from a tall glass of water that sat on the edge of the bathtub next to four or five bottles of shampoo, which she used in rotation. She could disappear with her camera for hours, particularly in thunderstorms. Her shift at the restaurant ended no later than midnight but on stormy nights she came home at three or four in the morning, hair plastered to her forehead, soaked to the skin. He would have suspected her of cheating in those times except that it was clear from the condition of her clothing that she hadn't been indoors all night, and later he'd see the pictures she'd taken, streetscapes of rain and lightning with trees bending in the wind. She'd extract herself from layer upon sodden layer of clothing, happy and shivering and her skin cold to the touch, and then she'd spend an hour or so in a steaming-hot shower and sleep in until at least noon. She had no explanation for these evenings except that she liked walking in rainstorms and her camera was waterproof. He was desperately curious but never asked where she went. He tried not to press her for too many details, about her scars or her family or anything else; she'd come from nowhere and seemed to have no past, and it seemed possible, even in the beginning when everything was easy, that the tenuous logic of her existence in his life might collapse under close examination. He didn't want to know.

"What I want," she said quietly, on the third night he spent with her, "is to stop travelling and stay in the same place for a while. I'm starting to think I've been travelling too much."

And for Eli—frustrated, aimless, working at a job he didn't particularly like, failed scholar, unable to decide what to do with his life—the idea of *travelling too much* was unimaginably exotic, and he pulled her close and fucked her again and imagined staying beside her forever. But that was only the third night she spent with him.

She was easily distracted. She had a photographer's fascination with quality of light. An upside-down CD reflecting rainbows on the bedroom ceiling, a glass of red wine catching the light of a candle, the Empire State Building piercing white against the sky at night. Violently beautiful sunsets could reduce her to tears. She was virtually incapacitated by fireflies. She was sublimely abnormal, and very frequently unnerving, but she was his psalm. What a live-in lover offers you, ultimately, is the unprecedented revelation of not being alone. She slipped so easily into the folds of his life. Her few belongings vanished into his apartment.

It always seemed later on that he loved her, at least partially, because she rendered him fraudulent. He talked about travelling, but she had travelled. He talked about photography, but she took photographs. He talked about languages, but she translated them. He felt that if she were a screenwriter she'd write screenplays instead of talking about screenplays and sketching outlines of screenplays and analyzing screenplays the way Thomas did. If she were a painter, he felt that she'd paint. What he liked best were the times when they went into the café and none of his friends were there, so they could sit together and read the paper in blissful silence. Or the afternoons when he sat at his desk and measured sentences, written and then deleted in equal measure, or did research while she sat in the armchair nearby and studied Russian texts, her lips moving soundlessly over the words. And life settled into a state not far from perfection, until he found the lists.

One: a list of names, ten pages, beginning and ending with *Lilia*. Most names had arrows that trailed out into the margins, where the names of places were noted in small print: *Mississippi, south Kansas, central Florida, Detroit.* Two: a list of words in a number of languages, which could've meant anything at all. He recognized the Spanish word for *butterfly* and the German word for *night—mariposa, nacht—*but the rest were incomprehensible to him. Like the list of names, the paper looked old and the handwriting was evolutionary; the beginning parts of both lists were in awkward childish block letters, which became smaller and more refined as the lines progressed. Three: a list of words and phrases. This third list was longer and of a different genre; no evolutionary transformation was in evidence, and all the languages represented were ailing or dead. He recognized whole phrases from his notebooks. These pages were uncrumpled and new-looking. He went through this last list over and over again but could detect no pattern in the phrases she'd copied. There were words from five continents. Her suitcase also contained six or seven books and a weathered business card for a private investigator in Montreal, but it was the lists that interested him.

"I was just collecting the words," she explained. "I didn't mean to plagiarize, I just liked the way they looked. I wanted to save them on the page," she said. "Like pressed flowers in a book."

He found this perfectly understandable. He liked patterns too. But the rest of it, my love, these other pages . . .

"I make lists," she said, stating the obvious. "I always did." He was pacing distractedly around the apartment. She sat in the armchair, regarding him quietly. She was interested to know why he'd gone through her suitcase in the first place.

He forced his voice to be steady. "I'm curious about the names."

She began to tell him a story in bed that night, a long story about deserts and aliases and driving away, motel pay phones and a blue Chrysler Valiant in the mountains. She spoke in measured tones, her hands moving ceaselessly over his skin. He listened, at first incredulous and then shocked into belief, but he wasn't too caught up in the words to notice that she was tracing the contours of wings over his shoulder blades.

4

There is a word in the Dakota language, gender-specific and untranslatable, that expresses the specific loneliness of mothers whose children are absent. Eli told Lilia the word once when they were lying in bed together, and it was hard not to think of her mother when she heard it.

Lilia's mother said once in an interview that she wished she could forget her daughter. (The interview aired on *Unsolved Cases*. It's on the internet somewhere, although Lilia can't quite bring herself to watch it again.) It was a cruel thing to say, but touchingly pragmatic. Lilia's mother had a daughter who disappeared: this is the kind of catastrophe that marks a person forever afterward, as indelibly as a missing limb.

On the night her daughter disappeared it was late November, and a heavy snowfall had blanketed the lawn. Just before Lilia left the house for the last time a sound startled her out of sleep, or perhaps she was lying awake already. When the sound came again she climbed out of bed and went to the window, the floorboards cold beneath her feet. She opened the window and the air outside was exquisitely cold, the lawn brilliant with snow and moonlight, and beyond the lawn the forest rose up like a wall. She saw her breath in the frozen air. Her father was standing in the snow beneath the window. He waved to her and smiled and pressed a finger to his lips. *Shh.* She turned back into the room, clutching her bunny (it was blue, and its eyes were startled round buttons that gleamed dark in the half-light), and she made her way out into the silent hall. A bare floorboard creaked softly as she passed her half-brother's room. He lay still, but he wasn't sleeping. He listened to her footsteps recede unsteadily on the stairs. Lilia skipped the ninth stair, which sometimes creaked, and tiptoed through moonlight on the landing, the banister railing at shoulder height. Down through the shadows of the living room, through the silent kitchen. She unlocked the front door and ran out barefoot into the snow.

Her father lifted her into his arms, and she dropped the bunny as her feet left the ground. *My lily*, he kept saying, *Lilia, my dove* . . . He hadn't seen her in almost a year and a half, but he remembered how to hold her so she wouldn't fall. He kept saying her name as he took her away from there, Lilia's bandaged arms around his neck and her heart beating fast against his shoulder, teeth chattering in the cold. She closed her eyes against his shoulder. He carried her quickly across the lawn and into the forest, where everything was silent and waiting and dark. The air was a little warmer here, and no snow penetrated the branches on the forest floor. The only snow here was on the driveway, a pale ribbon winding down between the trees. To her brother, watching from the window on the staircase landing, it was as though the forest closed behind them like a gate.

Far from the house, beyond the wall of the forest, a car started down by the road. Lilia's mother stirred uneasily in her sleep as it receded. Her brother turned away from the window and returned to his bed.

This was her escape. It was recorded in newspapers.

5

The morning after he found the lists, Eli left her sleeping and went alone to the café where he'd met her. He bought a coffee and a newspaper and took a seat in the corner, trying to sink into the clatter of voices and coffee cups. He spent a few minutes staring at the date on his newspaper before he glanced at the headlines, hoping that reading today's date in typeface might have a steadying effect. He reread the front page a few times but couldn't concentrate on it well enough to open the first section. He turned to Arts and Leisure: certain musicals were sweeping Broadway and might stay there forever, certain others were failing and would soon disappear, some films were brilliant and others were not, and none of it seemed to matter much. He refolded the paper and looked for a while at the print of Icarus on the opposite wall, trying to decipher her by association, but Icarus persisted in falling through the clueless blue. Eli pulled his notebook out of his bag and then put it back in. He abandoned his coffee and went back to the apartment.

She wasn't there, and he wondered about her whereabouts through a torturous day. She came back in the evening and was vague about where she'd been, as always. She'd been at a bookstore, she said, and then a park, and then walking, and then another park, and before all that she'd seen Geneviève on the street. Lilia didn't like Geneviève very much and suspected this was mutual, but when Geneviève was fired up about something she couldn't restrain herself from discussing it with the first person she happened to come across, so she'd swept Lilia into the nearest café.

"It was almost malicious," Lilia said. "I kept on having to order things because we were there for so long. She talked about string theory through two cups of coffee and a scone, and I still don't really know what string theory is."

"It involves strings." He was tired. "I think they sort of waver."

He sat on the couch and pulled her close to him, relieved and peaceful and restless in equal measure, while she asked about the wavering. He didn't know, he just had an idea that they wavered. Metaphorically wavered? Were they metaphorical strings? He wasn't sure. Maybe. She should look it up. He didn't know much about physics. Actually, he didn't know *anything* about—she didn't even *like* scones, she said, interrupting him. They were just there, and she couldn't bring herself to drink another cup of coffee. But it was a good afternoon, she said, despite Geneviève; she'd found a Russian edition of *Delirious Things*. He'd never heard of it. She repeated the title in Russian, taking obvious pleasure in what he could only assume was an impeccable pronunciation, and got up to show it to him. The Cyrillic alphabet spiked inscrutably at him from the cover above an artfully blurry black-and-white photograph that may or may not have depicted a girl in a nightgown walking over hot coals, or perhaps walking on water. It was Great Russian Literature, she said. In the absence of any knowledge of Russian, he was in no position to contest this.

"It's late," he said finally. He'd been holding her on the couch while she lapsed into quiet, flipping through the first few pages. He was half asleep, almost dreaming, her warmth against him. He was breathing the scent of her latest shampoo, like cinnamon and violets.

Later he lit a candle in the bedroom and she lay beside him staring up at the ceiling. Sleep was out of the question. He waited, and after a while she began to speak again. Last night's story, continued. A trajectory of cities, of places, of names. He wondered if she was telling the truth. There was no reason to suspect that she wasn't. Her voice was nearly expressionless. *I used to see mirages in the desert. Pools of water on the highway. We were driving in a small grey car* . . . She twisted onto her side, facing him, and her hand cupped the bone of his hip. A long stroke down the outside of his thigh. *It was shadowless. I think the sand was almost white. We'd been driving for so long, and there was another car behind us* . . . She trailed off mid-sentence, stopped the motion of her hand. He held her close and touched her hair, kissed her softly on the forehead, *Lilia, Lilia, it's all right, shh* . . . but she wasn't upset, just absent, and he felt that she was slipping away from him. She smiled in the candlelight, but her eyes were unfocused. *We must have driven through a thousand towns that year, and then we came into Cincinnati at night* . . .

He woke from a fitful dream of cars and deserts, a twilight kind of sleep. She was breathing beside him in the light of first morning, an arm extended over the tangle of sheets. Her lips were parted slightly, and he could see the movement of her eyes beneath her lids. Eli wondered what she was dreaming of. He got up without waking her and went back to the café. The coffee was strong there, but the newspaper was failing him again, and he was still dazed and only half awake when he left. How could a story throw everything off so suddenly, so clearly? He felt the foundations breaking apart beneath them.

He found Thomas and Geneviève in another café and sat with them for a while trying to lose himself in pointless arguments, and then went to the gallery for an utterly uneventful shift. When he came home in the late afternoon she was in the bathroom. Judging by the razor blades on the edge of the bathtub, she'd long since finished shaving her legs. Now she sat cross-legged in a foot of bathwater, removing her pubic hair with a pair of tweezers. This apparently required her complete attention. She barely glanced up at him when he entered the room. He'd seen her do this before, and it always unnerved him. He sat on the toilet lid.

"That can't possibly be making you happy," he said.

She smiled.

"It makes me wince to look at it. Are you all right?"

"Fine," she said pleasantly. "I'm fine. Thank you."

"That . . . that doesn't . . ." He gestured toward her, but she didn't look at him.

"What?"

"That, uh, that doesn't hurt?"

"Oh," she said. "No, not really."

"It seems a bit obsessive, don't you think?"

She didn't reply.

He rested his elbows on his knees, clasped his hands in front of him, and stared between his wrists at the white tiled floor.

"I was just at work," he said, "a little while ago. No one came into the gallery. It was just me standing there, staring at the walls."

She was looking at him.

"I had some time on my hands, and I was thinking about your story. And I couldn't help but . . . I was thinking about your story," Eli said, "and I would be lying if I said it didn't frighten me a little."

She didn't spe . Her face betrayed nothing. The small movements of her hand continued, silver tweezers distorted by ripples. The water was a lucid green.

"More than a little. The fact that you were abducted would be something unusual in itself, but it's just . . . it's just," he said, "that you always seem to leave. All of your stories are about you leaving."

It gradually became clear that she wasn't going to answer him.

"On the way home I bought you a pomegranate." He leaned forward quickly to kiss her forehead and then sat back down on the toilet lid with her sweat on his lips.

"Thank you," said Lilia. "That was nice of you."

He watched her for a while in silence.

"Why do you like them so much?"

"Like what?"

"Pomegranates."

"Oh." There was a long pause, during which she became methodically more hairless. He was watching the point where the water touched her skin. Her limbs were slightly tanned, but the rest of her was a few shades paler. White stomach, green water, silver metal in her hand moving under the surface distorted by ripples, the meditative rhythm of her movements. She didn't seem quite human; a pale clean-shaven creature, half mermaid, half girl. *My aquatic love.* The water, as always, was far too hot. A bead of sweat left a trail between her breasts. She looked slippery. "I don't know," she said, "I've just always liked them."

"Are you evasive about everything?"

But she wouldn't be drawn into an argument; she stopped tweezing, reached for the glass of water on the edge of the bathtub, sipped at it, held it to her forehead for a second, returned it to precisely the place where it had been before and took up the tweezers again, all without looking at him.

Eli couldn't avoid the question anymore. He kept his voice as steady as possible and didn't lift his gaze from the floor.

"I need to know if you're going to leave me."

She stopped then and set the tweezers beside the half-empty glass. She clasped her hands in the water and sat for a moment looking down at them.

"I don't know," she said.

He stood up slowly and left the room. The apartment seemed foreign to him. He walked back and forth across the floor a few times, swiped his hand across his eyes, stood with his arms crossed in front of a window. He sat at his desk for a few minutes and then stood up again, opened a few books that he immediately closed, and finally settled on opening the window to the fire escape. Someone had left a book on the windowsill. He threw *Delirious Things* as far as he could into the empty air, realized what he was doing as the book left his hand and tried to catch it, too late; he swore softly and climbed out the window and spent some time looking for it from the fire-escape landing, peering down over the railing, but he couldn't see it on the street below. He sat out there for a while longer, hoping someone below might pick it up and exclaim loudly enough for him to hear, at which point he could do something useful. People walked alone or in groups on the pavement, drove toward the Williamsburg Bridge or away from it, rode bicycles and carried on conversations. Laughter carried up to the level of the fire escape. An airplane passed silently overhead. No one below seemed to pick up a book. Eli only went back inside when the sun began to drop below the level of the rooftops. A cold breeze was drifting off the river.

The apartment was silent. He found her in the bathtub, sitting cross-legged and staring down at her hands, the water grown cool around her. She was shivering, and it seemed she hadn't moved since he left.

"I threw your book out the window," he said. "I'm sorry."

She murmured something inaudible.

"I didn't mean to," he said. "I'm sorry, I don't know why I did it. I just don't want you to leave."

"I know," she whispered. "It's not that I want to, Eli, it's just that I've always . . ."

"You've always what?"

"Try to imagine what it's like," she said. "I don't know how to stay."

"Come here." He pulled her up out of the bathtub, threw a towel over her shoulders, and held her close to him. He could feel her heartbeat against his chest. She let her head fall on his shoulder, and the cold water in her hair seeped through to his skin. She let herself be led to the bedroom by his hand around her wrist; her pulse didn't register against his fingertips. She eased herself down onto the bed, still without looking at him, and he saw that there were tears on her face. She pulled the duvet over her head and curled away from him.

Eli left her there. In the kitchen he found the pomegranate he'd bought for her and quartered it quickly on a pale blue plate. He thought the contrast between the shades of the pomegranate and the blue might please her. Any one of a number of details can prevent a ship from sinking. He carried the plate back to the bedroom and set it on the bedside table to grope for the flashlight under the bed. He took off his shoes, his belt, his jeans, left them in a heap on the floor, held the flashlight between his teeth and climbed under the duvet like a man entering a cave. He reached out for the blue plate and then turned to her, and her face was illuminated in the dimness.

"Don't leave me," he whispered. "Stay, I'll buy you pomegranates. I won't throw any more of your books out the window, I promise."

She smiled faintly, still in tears.

"Here," he said, "hold the flashlight."

She sat up and took it from him, the duvet a tent between their heads. He sat cross-legged with the plate on his lap and tore the pomegranate apart, juice running down his hands and wrecking the sheets. He began to feed her pomegranate beads, two or three at a time, and she stopped weeping long before her lips were stained red.

6

Lilia left her mother's house a little after midnight. Her half-brother Simon was the first one downstairs in the morning. He woke, shivering, just before dawn. A cold breeze filled the house; the front door, closed imperfectly, had blown open after Lilia had left, and also a kitchen window was broken. There was ice in the glass of water on his bedside table.

He climbed out of bed and pulled his quilt over his shoulders like a cloak. It trailed heavily behind him down the stairs, gathering dust. He almost immediately lost feeling in his toes. The kitchen door was wide open, and snow had drifted over the threshold. At that hour the air outside was suffused with the greyish light that comes over northern landscapes just before the sun rises, when everything seems tired and somewhat unreal. Simon stood just inside the door, clutching the quilt around his shoulders and staring out at the lawn, and even though the scene outside was exactly what he'd been expecting, he found at that moment that he needed his mother, and also that he couldn't speak. He reached outside, around the door frame, and began ringing the doorbell over and over again.

She was by his side almost instantly and then running back up the stairs. He stood still in the doorway, listening to her footsteps in the upstairs hall, the sound she made when she saw that Lilia's bedroom was empty. She was on the phone a moment later, although it took the dispatcher at the police station a few minutes to understand what she was saying. She called the more recent of her two ex-husbands and screamed obscenities into his answering machine until the machine cut her off. She hung up, shaking, and stared at her son. Her face was white. He met her gaze and looked quickly away. He was briefly interested to notice that he could see his breath inside the house.

"She dropped her bunny," he said. His voice was stunned. "And there's still glass in the snow."

The kitchen window had been broken the night before, and glass was still shining on the snow outside. She stared at the shattered window for a moment.

"Help me," she whispered. "Put your shoes on. Bring me the broom." He pulled his boots on over his pyjamas and let the quilt fall on the kitchen floor, and they worked together for a while in feverish silence, scooping and sweeping the broken glass out of the snow, collecting it into a shoebox from the hall closet. When they were done the cuffs of his pyjamas were cold and soaking wet against his wrists. In the kitchen doorway she turned to him suddenly—he flinched and raised an arm reflexively to protect his face—but she only placed the box of broken glass and snow in his arms. The cardboard was soggy.

"Hide this," she said, in a tone of voice that he knew not to question, "and bring me a ball."

"What ball?" He was too dazed to cry.

"Any kind of ball, Simon. Wait . . ."

She went to the cupboard and took out three bottles of Scotch, one almost empty. She laid these carefully on top of the snow and broken glass, and said, "Quickly, quickly."

He took the box to the woodshed and put it under an upside-down mouldering armchair. There was an old basketball on the woodshed floor, half deflated. When he brought it to her she was taping cardboard over the window, standing on the kitchen chair that had been Lilia's only last night, weeping, talking to herself, taping fast. He went upstairs and dressed quietly, with a feeling of tremendous formality. He put on the pants he wore only on special occasions, a sweater that smelled of dust, and his good shoes.

He combed his hair without being told to, although he wasn't tall enough to see his whole head in the mirror. A short time later the police were there. They filled the kitchen with blue uniforms and tracked dirty snow into the house and fanned out to photograph what was there on the lawn. Not the lawn under the window, which had clearly been broken a day or two earlier. Simon, the mother explained through tears and hysterics, had been throwing a basketball in the house. See, there was the basketball, half buried in snow. She told them that she'd long since cleaned up the glass, that someone was coming to replace the window. They nodded, uninterested. They were photographing a spot beyond that, farther out toward the driveway and slightly to the right. It's the perfect photograph: a child's bare footprints emerge from the house, clearly visible in the snow, and meet after a few steps with the prints of a man's winter boots. This is the point where the blue knitted bunny lies whitened by frost, and here there's a scuff in the snow where she was swept off her feet. The bootprints turn here and recede into the forest and eventually coincide, some distance outside the frame of the photograph, with the tire marks down by the road.

The bunny was briefly famous, in a localized way. A couple of regional newspapers showed pictures of it staring up at the sky. Simon was the one who retrieved it that afternoon, when the photographers were done taking pictures. He put it in the bathtub for a while and sat on the bathtub's edge to watch the pool of bluish water oozing out around it, then put it through the dryer. He sat in front of the dryer on an upturned milk crate, watching it spinning around and around. It came out hot but still wet, so he put it back in the dryer and watched it blurring around again until he got dizzy and had to look away. His mother was sobbing and sobbing in the kitchen, talking about Lilia and Lilia's father and how she always just knew he was going to do something like this and that was why she had gotten the restraining order in the first place, and there were police officers everywhere. Some wanted to speak to him. He answered questions in a polite monotone, lying mostly, and when they were finished with him he took the bunny upstairs to his room and set it up on a folded towel on the corner of the bed. It still wasn't completely dry, but he didn't want to be downstairs anymore.

His mother came to him in the evening, when almost everyone had gone. There was a social worker in the kitchen and someone from the police station rigging something to the telephone, and there was a car down by the road with two police officers in it. She sat on the edge of his bed and stared tearfully at him. He wouldn't meet her eyes.

"Thank you for helping me with the glass," she said.

IN A MOTEL ROOM three hundred miles to the south, Lilia's father was cutting off her hair. In the very beginning her arms had gauze bandages on them, for reasons that were almost immediately unclear. She sat on a chair in the bathroom and watched dark curls falling past her face and landing on the bandages, on the floor, on her legs, while her father moved around her with the scissors.

"Hold still, now," he said gently, although she hadn't been moving. She didn't answer, but she did wrinkle her nose at the smell of bleach. It hurt much more than she had thought it would. She winced and tried to ignore the smell and the tingling while he stood close beside her and kept up a soothing, uninterrupted monologue: "Did I ever tell you, my dove, about the time I was working as a magician in Vegas? This was at a place called La Carnivale, one of the big old casinos, and . . ." And she didn't say anything, but he didn't expect her to. She never could remember why they'd left in the first place, but she did remember that in the first year of travelling she didn't say very much. She was unmoored and her memories were eroding in the sunlight, and she was rendered shy by the strangeness of this fast new life. He was driving south.

He would talk to her whether she'd talk to him or not, and it was his voice that gradually put her at ease. He could talk about types of stone, about Goya's black paintings or the magnificent staircase in Rembrandt's *Philosopher in Meditation*, about genetics: the specific signatures of persistent genes, replicating themselves endlessly through the diluting generations. When she grew quiet and despondent, which was often in the beginning, he liked to save her with a fact. Did you know that my favourite composer went deaf at the height of his career? Did I ever tell you about the moons of Jupiter? There's this one in particular that's covered in ice . . . She didn't know him well in the very beginning, but she was profoundly soothed by the sound of his voice. On this particular night, twenty hours after he'd lifted her from the snow, he was talking about the arcing bridge in Monet's garden, the way it changed, over the passage of the painter's career, from sharpness into an almost abstract vagueness. "Think of that," he was saying. "An object changing in the manner of a memory." He rubbed her burning head with a towel. *"Et voilà!"* he said. "Brace yourself, my dove, this will be startling . . ." and he held Lilia up to the motel bathroom mirror.

The effect was shocking. She remembered that moment as the first time she ever looked in a mirror and didn't recognize herself. A strange child with short dishevelled blond hair stared back at her, and she felt suddenly, inexplicably safe. Not only safe but elated, the first time true happiness ever coursed through her chest, like the breaking open of a gate.

"You like it?"

She smiled.

"I'm glad you approve. Now you just need a new name," he said.

The first false name was Gabriel, chosen because with short hair she looked very much like a boy, and he figured a little ambiguity couldn't hurt. Still, the name didn't seem fraudulent. She couldn't help but feel that Gabriel was just as real as Lilia, and as real as the dense parade of phantoms that followed: after Gabriel she was Anna, and she was Michelle, Laura, Melissa, and Ruth by spring. In retrospect her childhood was all false names and lost memories. The more time passed, the harder it was to say what was real and what wasn't. There were scars on her arms for which she had no explanation.

7

"What was the book about?" Eli asked sleepily. "What were the delirious things?"

They were lying together under the pomegranate-stained sheets, the blue plate broken somewhere at the foot of the bed, and he'd been apologizing again for throwing her book out the window. Now that it was gone, he was curious about it.

"They were memories." Her voice was languid. "The way they go all hazy when you stare at them too long." After some time had passed he pressed for more details, but she'd fallen asleep. Breathing lightly against his arm.

It was never very easy to reach her, like loving someone who was rarely in the same room. But it would have been difficult to imagine, in a purely abstract sense, a girl more perfect; he'd had to concede shortly after she'd moved in with him that she was no less interested in his field of study than he was. He lived quietly alongside his work, he couldn't imagine being separated from it, he wanted to know as much about it as possible, he thought about it now and then through the course of any given hour in the day. But she was caught up in it, she was dancing with it, she was having a fling. She understood the poetry of multiplicity, of estrangement, of irreconcilable concepts of geography: in one of the Mayan languages there are nine different words for the colour blue. (He'd been aware of this for years, but she was the one who made him wonder what all those untranslatable shades of blue might look like.) In Wintu, a language of ancient California, there are no words for *right* and *left*: speakers differentiate between *riverside* and *mountainside*, from a time when it was taken as a given that you would live your life and bear children and die in the landscape where you and your parents and your great-great-grandparents had been born. A language that would disintegrate at sea, or while travelling beyond either the river or mountains; go beyond the boundaries and there would be no reference points, no words to describe the landscape you moved through—imagine the unfathomable cost of leaving home. Or the Australian Guugu Yimithir, a language of ferociously absolute positioning, in which there was no way to tell someone, for instance, that Lilia is standing to your left; you'd have to say, instead, "Lilia is standing to the west of me." In that language there are no variables, only north, south, east, west. If that were the only language you had ever known, would it be possible to think in relative terms, in terms of variables, directionlessness, things that are changeable and a little delirious rather than certain, mirages, shades of grey? She read deep into his books and surfaced with questions, and he read to her sometimes aloud from his notes: *"I dream in Chamicuro,"* the last fluent speaker of her language told a reporter, in her thatched-hut village in the Peruvian jungle in the final year of the twentieth century, *"but I cannot tell my dreams to anyone. Some things cannot be said in Spanish. It's lonely being the last one."*

He looked up from his notebook and there were tears in her eyes. If the dreams of the last speaker of Chamicuro won't survive the passage into another language, then what else has been lost? What else that was expressible in that language cannot be said in another? A language disappears, on average, every ten days. Last speakers die, words slip into memory, linguists struggle to preserve the remains. What every language comes down to, at the end, is one last speaker. One speaker of a language once shared by thousands or millions, marooned in a sea of Spanish or Mandarin or English. Perhaps loved by many but still profoundly alone;

reluctantly fluent in the language of her grandchildren, but unable to tell anyone her dreams. How much loss can be carried in a single human frame? Their last words hold entire civilizations.

In the language of the Hopi tribe, there is no differentiation between past, present, and future tense. The divisions do not exist. "What does that do to time?" he asked one night, half drunk on red wine. They had long since closed their books for the evening. He was running his fingertips over her collarbone, tracing that little hollow just below her throat with his thumb. It was already October. She would be gone in a week.

"No," she said softly, "what does it do to free will?"

He was preoccupied with kissing her neck and didn't immediately understand what she meant. But he couldn't fall asleep that night, and when the understanding finally hardened and crystallized, hours later, it was enough to jolt him out of bed. He sat for a long time in the darkened living room, wide awake, listening to her breathing in the adjoining room.

What does it do to free will? *You disappeared. You are disappearing. You will disappear.* If there is a language in which all those sentences are the same, then who are we to say that they're different?

ON THE EVENING of Lilia's disappearance Eli sat at his desk for hours, trying to read at first, then staring at his computer screen, and then just staring at his hands. I surrender. She either didn't hear this thought or heard it and still didn't come home. He taped a white napkin to the inside of the bedroom window, the only window that faced the street. He would have done anything. It was the closest thing he had to a flag. When the trick-or-treaters had gone he returned to his desk, and the hours slid away from him. Five in the morning: cold grey light. By night's end the apartment seemed like an illusion. She was here a moment ago, in the bed, in the shower, her towel on the floor of the bedroom is still damp, none of this can possibly be real. He fell asleep at dawn with his head on his arms, listening for her footsteps, and slept in this position again the next night. Two days passed before he could bring himself to even look at the bed. The rumpled duvet still held the shape of her body.

The day after she left he bought a map of the continent. He remembered every location she'd told him in her story and he circled the cities she'd passed through in red, looking for a pattern, looking for the next city along the line. If there was a way to find her, he would. He had an idea that if he stared at the map long enough, he might possibly be able to divine where she had gone.

8

Lilia's father had purchased a map at an all-night gas station, on his way through the darkness to his ex-wife's house, a few hours before the abduction. When she was seven Lilia liked to trace the ink-line ridges of mountains with her fingertips and admire the patterns made by highways across the continental United States. When she was eight he taught her how to read the map, and by nine she was the navigator. When he showed her how it all worked (north, border, highway, town) she asked where on the map they'd started, but her father shook his head and said, "It's not important, kiddo, you've got to live in the present." She took enormous pleasure in reading maps. Every town, to her way of thinking, held an alternate life. She liked to close her eyes and touch a spot on the map, open her eyes and move her finger to the nearest place name, and sketch out the future she might have there as he drove: "We should go to Lafoy, and buy a house, and get a library membership and a cat and a dog, and then start a restaurant—"

"What kind of restaurant?"

"The kind that serves ice cream."

"But then we'd have to stay in Lafoy," her father said. "We'd have a house."

"I don't want to stop." This was true, she didn't, and she'd been writing messages in motel Bibles to this effect for over a year now. Lilia saw motel Bibles as a kind of bulletin board, where messages might be left for other travellers following behind. When she was nine Lilia and her father lived together, a unit, in the same motel room or in the same small car, and the messages in motel Bibles were almost her only secret. She scrawled them furtively while her father was in the shower, taking pleasure in the idea that he wouldn't approve. The shred of privacy afforded by having a secret somehow seemed about as close as she'd ever come to having her own room.

"In that case, kiddo, better come up with a new plan."

"Let's drive *through* Lafoy, and go to the library, and then stay at a motel, and then go to a restaurant and have ice cream, and then leave again."

"I like that plan much better," her father said.

Their lives were easiest in the summer, when they didn't have to make up explanations for why Lilia wasn't in school and there were other children to play with in the parks. They camped for months at a time when it was warm enough. A week at one campground, a week somewhere else. She liked camping, although it took her a long time to fall asleep in campgrounds. There was sometimes rain on the roof of her tent, and it rendered the night mysterious and full of hidden sounds. In campgrounds she heard footsteps, or sometimes the sounds of trains in the distance; lie still and she could hear the night trains passing, carrying freight between the prairies and the seas. They hiked in national parks and went to outdoor concerts in small towns. Her father loved music of almost any kind. He would drive for hours to reach concerts in parks and summer music festivals, where they'd sit on the grass with bottles of lemonade and sandwiches.

It was harder in the wintertime. They tried to stay in the Southern states during the school year because Lilia's father hated cold weather and Lilia liked both the desert and the places with palm trees, but the explanations were more difficult. Sometimes when she got tired of lying about being home-schooled she'd stay in the motel room until three o'clock in the afternoon, reading books that her father brought her from a bookstore or working on the mathematics problems that he came up with for her. In the late afternoons they went to the movies, to a mall for ice cream, to a museum if there was one, to a park if it was warm enough. Her father insisted that she learn to swim, and to this end they stayed for nearly five months in a town near Albuquerque while she took a full course of after-school swimming lessons at the local pool. Strange being in the same place for so long. By the time she was good enough to dive from the high diving board and swim laps, she was skittish and uneasy and not sleeping well at night. The day after her first swim meet, her father suggested that they go somewhere else, and she was happy to get back in the car and drive away again.

Her father didn't like stopping for long in any one place, even after the first frantic year when capture seemed most imminent. Her father knew about endless travel, and he wanted to show her everything he knew. He had been born to American diplomats in Colombia, started high school in Bangkok, finished it in Australia, and then moved to the United States. He'd spent the next few years earning multiple degrees from a random sampling of universities, too restless to settle on any one of them; afterward he'd worked for a few months as an adjunct professor of languages until an unfortunate incident involving an undergrad who'd looked much older than seventeen had put an abrupt halt to his academic career. He'd worked as a shipping clerk for a while after that, taught himself to write software at night, served six months in a minimum-security prison for some complicated counterfeiting scheme that he was never inclined to explain in any great detail except to remark that obviously it hadn't worked out very well, been employed for some time as a bartender in a hotel in Las Vegas, married Lilia's mother, and was divorced from her by the time Lilia was three. She was, he said, an impossible woman. He wouldn't tell Lilia what was specifically impossible about her mother, although he did show her a small scar below his left cheekbone from the time

Lilia's mother had thrown a telephone at his head. In the four years between the thrown telephone and the night he'd appeared on the lawn beneath Lilia's bedroom window, he'd made a minor fortune on the stock market.

In the beginning her father drove and kept driving because it was necessary to flee quickly, but later it seemed to Lilia that eventually they probably could have stopped. Ceased their endless driving after enough time had passed, perhaps settled in some anonymous town when she was ten or eleven, somewhere far from where they had begun. Changed her name one last time, enrolled her in an elementary school with the help of a forged birth certificate, settled into a quiet, almost ordinary life. (And Lilia could almost see this other life at times, like a scene playing out on the other side of a gauze curtain, dim but glimpsable: the first quiet years of elementary school and forgetting, kissing boys in cars parked at lookout spots, a front porch with flowers planted in the backs of plastic swans, her father recast eventually as the slightly eccentric but kindly grandfather smoking his pipe on the front steps and lending his lawn mower to the neighbours, and the early upheaval so distant that she's no longer sure it wasn't a dream. *My mother died when I was born*, she tells her sympathetic future husband on a quiet night in August, believing it enough herself that it doesn't even feel like a lie anymore, and a passing jet leaves a sunset-coloured trail across the sky.)

But they didn't stop. He was afraid, he told her much later, that if the two of them paused too long anywhere, especially in the early days, she'd start to dwell on the increasing strangeness of her upbringing, the missing parts of her family, events that may or may not have transpired just before he'd taken her away. There were weeks that were mostly spent driving, singing along with her father in a car passing over an infinity of highways, making friends with waitresses in small-town cafés, conjugating Italian verbs in motel rooms from California to Vermont and then Spanish all the way back west again. Her father regretted that he couldn't send her to school, he said, but to make up for it he wanted to teach her all the languages he knew. In the glove compartment they carried a battered prayer card for St. Brigid of Ireland, the patron saint of fugitives. Lilia's father wasn't religious but said the prayer card couldn't hurt.

This was a skittish life, but Lilia was unusually calm. Nothing could startle her. She was profoundly unafraid, although there were near-disasters: when she escaped from the motel in Cincinnati, police rapping on the door of the motel room as she squeezed out the bathroom window and dropped down into the wet grass and then climbed through a dark hedge and sprinted, her frantic father waiting in the parking lot of a gas station half a block away, she was calm all the rest of that night. Her father asked if she was scared, and she said she was too old to be afraid of things. She knew something about getting older. She was almost ten and a half. And it was true that her voice was tense when she asked if the police were still close, but it was also true that she was asleep within a couple of hours. Her father that night was scattered and frantic, driving fast but trying not to speed, looking in the mirror for flashing lights and glancing sideways at his daughter, fraught with directionless guilt, trying to drive away quickly and take care of her and let her be all at once. Hours out of Cincinnati he said something and she didn't answer, and in the passing lights of automobiles he saw that she'd fallen asleep. He tuned the radio to a classical music station, Chopin and then Mendelssohn with the volume low, night lullabies, and he hummed softly to the music and drove all through the night.

9

Four weeks after Lilia left, at the end of November, Eli received a postcard from Montreal. There was no return address. The front depicted a pretty line of grey stone houses with flowerboxes and iron staircases that spiralled from the second floors down to the street, with *Montréal* in drop-shadowed italics across the bottom. The back held a peculiar message, scrawled in what very clearly wasn't Lilia's hand-writing: *She's here. Come to Club Electrolite on Rue Ste.-Catherine, and raise a white flag on the dance floor. I'll see you. Come here soon. Michaela.*

If the whole business of life on earth had ever made sense to him, it ceased to at that moment. She unmoored him, her departure made him want to disappear, et cetera—but if the world was askew in the time after he met her, in the time after she left, the postcard spun it entirely from its axis. The day at the gallery passed like a dream. He took the postcard to the usual café, where Thomas had been camped out for two weeks trying to pick up a new waitress. Thomas stared at the postcard, whistled softly and shook his head.

"What would you do?" Eli felt fairly unhinged.

"I'd tear up the postcard and go find another girl. Or if you can't do that, at least forget about this one."

"What if she needs help?"

"What if she doesn't? This isn't a ransom note, it's just a weird message on the back of an ugly postcard. What if this is some kind of sick joke she's pulling, some ploy to get you back?"

"I have to go to her."

"No, you have to move on. What kind of a person

disappears like that? Look, things happen. Life continues. So you had a girlfriend who left."

"Easy for you to—"

"You think no one's ever left me? You can't chase after them," Thomas said. "When they leave like that, they're screwed up, and when they're screwed up, you can't save them. You can't save them. You just have to let them go." He made an airplane-like letting-go motion with one hand, jetting off to the left. "You just have to put your life back together and move on and let them do whatever it is they couldn't do with you around. It's the way it is."

"Thomas, this isn't her handwriting. Leave aside the fact that she left me, I have a postcard that someone's written about her from a foreign city."

"She left you, and you want to go *find* her?"

"I just want to make sure she's okay. I know she left me and she's probably a little crazy, it's just, I don't think she has anyone else."

"She might be *with* someone else, have you considered that? Some other guy could just . . . Eli, I'm sorry, wait . . ."

Eli stood and pulled his coat from the back of his chair. Out through the warmth of the café, Thomas calling after him, and outside night was falling and it was far too cold. He had a frantic desire to get out of Williamsburg, out of Brooklyn altogether, and found himself walking quickly toward the L-train stairs. There was a girl playing a guitar on the subway platform, sitting on a folding stool. She was singing soft songs about love and pay phones, almost to herself, until the sound of the oncoming train cancelled everything. In the crowd that spilled out through the train doors, there was an old woman pulling a little boy by the hand. The boy had a harmonica and played a long, wavering note in a minor key as Eli stepped into the train. He sank down onto a plastic bench and stared up at an overlit advertisement for skin care ("Dr. Z sees every patient personally!") for all of the long clattering journey under the river, and then up the stairs into the lights of Manhattan. He walked aimlessly down First Avenue against the wind.

He stopped at a Don't Walk signal somewhere deep in Chinatown, waiting for the direction of traffic to change. A bottle had been smashed in the gutter. He stood staring at it for a while, the mesmerizing sparkle of broken glass. A van paused a beat too long in the intersection and was attacked by a blaring cacophony of car horns. The sound brought tears to his eyes. He stood on the corner while passersby streamed around him like ghosts and lights changed from green to yellow to red to green again and the stream of traffic before him continued unchecked. He looked down and flecks of glass on the pavement sparkled, like crystal, like ice, tears blurring the pinpoints of light. It was a long time before he could force himself into motion.

"TELL ME ABOUT MONTREAL," he said to Geneviève. Thomas and Geneviève had been arguing earlier, but the argument was lost in passion and long words. Now they were both a bit flushed, mutually offended, and reading different sections of the same paper without speaking. Geneviève was making occasional notes in a weathered spiral-bound notebook. She had a scribbly, doctor's-prescription way of writing that produced long lines of cramped hieroglyphics, and he had been watching her write. It was the first thing he'd said in an hour.

"I thought maybe you'd forgotten how to talk," she said. "Why Montreal?" But her eyes held a sudden light. She loved talking about Montreal. She'd spent the early part of her life there. Her parents had moved her to Brooklyn when she was nine, but she still considered herself something of an expatriate and took enormous pleasure in pronouncing her name in French.

"I'm curious. I'm thinking about going there."

Thomas frowned. "Don't."

"Why not?" asked Geneviève, who didn't know about the postcard.

"Because it's fucking cold," Thomas said, without taking his eyes from Eli's face. "That's all anyone needs to know about it. You'd be insane to go there this time of year."

"I doubt you've even *been*." She was always ready to pounce on an opportunity to argue with anyone, but especially with Thomas. "You'd like it, Eli. It's a city with a probably doomed language. The Québécois are speaking French with an accent so ancient and frankly bizarre that French people from France can't understand it. It's like a fortress in a rising tide of English. It'll be like research for you."

"What do you mean, a fortress?"

"Imagine a country next to the sea," she said, "and imagine that the water's rising. Imagine a fortress that used to stand near the beach, but now it's half underwater, and the water won't stop rising no matter how they try to fight it back. Eventually, in the next century or so, it will more than likely rise over the top of the walls and overwhelm them, but for now they're plugging the cracks and pretending it doesn't exist and passing laws against rising water. I'm saying that French is the fortress, and English is the sea."

"I don't get it," said Thomas, without looking up from his paper. "That's a stupid metaphor."

"I think I do," said Eli quickly, trying to avoid losing them to another fight, but Geneviève had ignored Thomas anyway.

"You've spent your whole academic career thinking about dying languages," she said. "Thinking about doomed languages, shamelessly romanticizing doomed languages, picking up girls with doomed languages, and imagining what life played out in a doomed language might be like. Wouldn't you like to see what it really means to *live* in a city with a doomed language?"

"I would," he said. "I really would. Although I'm not sure that *career* is exactly the word for my academic situation. How cold is it?"

"Arctic," she said, "but it's worth it. There's no place like it on earth. I try to go back there every year. It's a great city." She was quiet for a moment. "Well," she said, "provided you speak French."

"What's *that* supposed to mean?" Thomas asked. He was still flushed and still wouldn't look up at her. "Eli, you can't chase them. We talked about this."

"Chase who? What are you talking about? What it means is certain laws are in place to protect the French language," she said. "Like I said, it's a fortress. Whether or not the scope of them is justified is somewhat controversial, but anyway, the English are more conservative, whereas the French . . ."

This sparked an instant argument on the subject of cultural stereotypes. They barely noticed when Eli walked out. There was a bad moment out on the street, where the fact of Lilia's absence slammed into his chest and he had to sit on a park bench for a while until the exhaustion lifted enough for him to stand up and get home. He spent the afternoon staring at the bedroom ceiling.

An envelope arrived the following morning. It was postmarked *Montreal*, and Queen Elizabeth II smiled against the sky-blue background of the stamp. The envelope contained a page torn from a Bible, with a child's awkward ballpoint-pen letters scrawled blue over the surface of the Twenty-second Psalm: *Stop looking for me. I'm not missing; I do not want to be found. I wish to remain vanishing. I don't want to go home.—Lilia.* The page was thin and slightly yellowed, and it trembled in his hands. There was nothing else in the envelope, but a phone number was scrawled on the inside of the flap with the message *Call me when you get to Montreal*, and he recognized the handwriting and the return address: Michaela, c/o Club Electrolite, a street number on Rue Sainte-Catherine. He was still staring at the envelope when the phone rang.

"Hello, Eli," his mother said.

He sank into the desk chair, closed his eyes, and lowered his forehead into the palm of his left hand. He clutched the phone white-knuckled with his right.

"Hi."

"You sound strange," she said. "Is everything okay?"

He told her that he was slightly tired. This seemed to be her cue. Did he know that it had been *two months* since he'd called her last? She was serious. Two *months!* She was only up in the Upper West *Side*, you know, not in *Siberia*, he *could* visit sometimes, or at least *call*, but *any*way. She just wanted to know how he was. How was the thesis coming? How was life in Brooklyn? She'd been out earlier, running a few errands, and on the way out of Zabar's she almost got hit by a taxi. On a crosswalk, on the walk signal! Manhattan taxi drivers are homicidal. She was thinking of writing to the mayor. But anyway, her friend Sylvia's daughter was having a baby—did he remember Sylvia's daughter? Red hair? Blue eyes? Yes, everyone was excited. She was the one who was right between Zed and Eli, agewise. And that bloody tap in the bathroom had begun dripping again, but she wasn't complaining. Because life's too short to complain about small things, especially if you're going to practically lose your life to a taxi on the way out of Zabar's, *c'est la vie*, et cetera.

She faded in and out, like a shifting and unreliable radio signal. The monologue eventually subsided, and silence settled over the line. Eli didn't speak.

She began speaking again all at once, fast and nervous. She just *worried* about him, she said, out there in the boroughs like that. She just didn't want him to end up like Zed. Eli transferred the phone into his left hand and held the torn page in his right. He turned the page over to read the rest of the psalm. *I am poured out like water, and all my bones are out of joint: my heart is like wax; it is melted in the midst of my bowels.* When he held it up to the window, Lilia's childhood handwriting was a backward shadow on the other side of the page. His mother wanted to know if he'd heard from Zed lately. At last word he was headed for Ethiopia, although she couldn't remember what he was doing there. It wasn't that she disapproved of Eli's brother, she wished he'd gone to college but she was proud of his humanitarian work, of course, glad he was seeing so much of the world (incidentally, had Eli considered travel? Maybe a month or two abroad would do him good, perhaps focus him a little), but she worried about Zed. She worried that Zed was getting too radical, too mystical (or was *spiritual* the right word? She was never sure what the difference was), just the way he wandered around biblical countries talking about *God* like that. Did he seem at all unhinged? Had he been heard from lately?

Eli turned the page over again. The first part of the psalm was partly lost under Lilia's handwriting, but he could still make it out: . . . *I cry in the day time, but thou hearest not; and in the night season, and am not silent.*

"No," he said, "I haven't heard from Zed for a while, but I don't think you should worry about him. He doesn't just talk about God, he talks about Buddhism and Taoism at least as much. What he suffers from—" He listened briefly to his mother's interruption for a second before he interrupted her. "No, he's not an extremist, you've got it all wrong. I was going to say what Zed suffers from is a pathological sense of democracy. He's too democratic to even choose one individual religion to be extreme and radical about. He's probably an atheist."

This last sentiment triggered a longish pause, in which he imagined her switching the telephone from one ear to the other and mentally rewriting her will.

"Eli," she said, "sweetheart, tell me what's wrong."

"I just don't think we're in any position to judge his life."

The pause lengthened and darkened. No, she told him, she was serious. She wanted to know what was wrong, with no diversions this time.

"My girlfriend disappeared." Eli listened for a moment and then interrupted her. "Yes, *Lilia*, the one I was living with, you think I'd have more than one? She didn't just leave me. I mean she disappeared."

His mother offered her opinion that girls don't just disappear, unless they've gone and gotten themselves—

"This one does."

Then she *did* go and get herself—

"No," he said, "she wasn't *preg*nant. For God's sake."

Her son, she felt, deserved better than that. And what did he mean by *disappeared*, exactly?

"She just got on a train and—"

"So she *left*."

"Yes, but it wasn't—"

"Then how do you know it was a train?"

"Because she said she was sick of travelling on buses," he said.

She was worried about him. How long had he been working on his thesis, out there in the boroughs? (She had a way of saying the word *boroughs* that conjured up images of far-off places of questionable repute: Uzbekistan, North Korea, Côte d'Ivoire.) How long was his thesis? It must be the length of *War and Peace* by this point. Was it even done yet? Wasn't it due a year ago, at least? Had he even turned in the proposal? Heaven knew she wasn't one to judge, of course, or to *criticize*, but he had to at least consider her point of view in this matter. It seemed a bit odd to her that he'd want to spend time chasing after noncommittal girls who leave on trains when here it had been years and he'd missed at least one thesis deadline already. What exactly was it that was so impossible to write about? He'd always been so good at writing, he'd always been so passionate about those dead languages of his, and she understood about writer's block, well, she *thought* she did, but how hard could it be? Well, she worried about him, that was all. He just seemed a bit lost to her when she called sometimes. Lacking focus. She just didn't want him to end up like Zed, wandering rootlessly through dangerous places far away. She still didn't understand why he didn't just finish his thesis and take his master's degree. She wondered sometimes if he knew what he wanted. She was afraid sometimes that perhaps he didn't.

He was reading the eleventh verse of the psalm: *Be not far from me; for trouble is near; for there is none to help.*

His mother was explaining about responsibility and adulthood. She had ideas about staying engaged with the world, as expressed in one's willingness to make something of one's life, particularly after having enjoyed the benefits of a lengthy and maternally funded university education. Which, naturally, was not an inexpensive proposition. Not that she *minded*, of course she didn't, not at all, and she certainly wasn't saying this to make him feel *guilty*, she just didn't want him to end up like his brother, she was just a bit concerned, and she wondered if he was fully aware of the—

"I know what I want," he said quietly. And suddenly, miraculously, the haze lifted. The decision was made. He let the phone drop a little, holding it loosely and barely listening to her, and with his other hand he was looking at a map on his phone. Montreal was less than an inch to the north.

She wanted to know what he meant by that, but he'd already hung up the phone. He reached for his wallet from the side table, folded the Bible page into it, grabbed his coat from the closet, and put his toothbrush and passport in opposite coat pockets. The telephone began ringing again within minutes, but he was already out the door.

PART TWO

10

In a low-lit jazz club in Montreal, some years before Eli arrived in the city, a detective was sitting alone at the bar. He was meeting an old friend, who was running late, and while he waited he examined his fedora in the dim light. His wife had given it to him for his birthday a month earlier, and it had an appealing newness about it. It was a perfect shade of chocolate brown. He rotated it slowly, admiring every angle, set it down on the gleaming dark wood of the bar, and ordered a pint of Guinness, which took some time to arrive.

He was trained in the reading of malevolent patterns. His work was essentially the study of intersections: the crosshairs where childhood trauma meets a longing for violence, where specific temperaments come up against messages written on mirrors in red lipstick, torn pairs of stockings in the empty industrial streets out by Métro Pie-IX, the backseats of second-hand automobiles and angles of moonlight over stains on concrete. He possessed a brilliant and sometimes eerie sense of intuition, which he wielded like a scalpel, and in the Montreal police department he was unsurpassed. His work usually involved rapists or murderers, and he had never worked with missing children until this particular afternoon at an almost deserted downtown jazz club, when his friend showed up forty-five minutes late, bought him a second beer to make up for it, and pulled a Bible out of his briefcase.

"Christopher," his friend said, "I need your help on something."

Christopher glanced at the Bible and then at Peter. "Don't tell me you've found religion," he said.

"No, this is evidence. Listen," Peter said, leaning forward a little, "have you ever thought about coming to work for me?"

"Thought never crossed my mind."

"You'd like working for me. You get a little more leeway to do your job. It's less . . . *procedural*, for lack of a better word. I don't believe in paperwork. But anyway, look, you don't have to decide right away about coming to work for me, I just want you to take a look at this. You know that parental abduction case I've been working on, the one I was telling you about?"

Peter opened the Bible on the bar. A certain page had been marked with a yellow sticky note.

A child's uneven handwriting sloped downward across the page in blue ink, overlapping the beginning of the Twenty-second Psalm: *Stop looking for me. I'm not missing; I do not want to be found. I wish to remain vanishing. I don't want to go home.—Lilia.*

"Good Lord," said the detective. He took the Bible from Peter's hands. "I could find her in ten minutes with something like this. How old did you say she was?"

"She's eleven and a half. Been missing a little over four years."

"Same age as my daughter. Missing from where?"

"Middle of nowhere, south of here. Her mother has a house to the south of here, not far from the American border. Her father's an American, so the kid has dual citizenship, and they'd probably crossed the border before the mother even reported her missing. Anyway, the girl's been missing for years, and the police've been useless. Someone recognized them from a poster and they almost caught her in Cincinnati a year ago, but nothing after that. There's just no trail. She could be anywhere this evening."

"This note is recent?"

"Not particularly. Some religiously inclined travelling salesman found it in his motel room in Toledo three years ago."

"Three years ago. So she was eight when she wrote this." He was still looking at the note, shaking his head. An image flashed through him—a small girl with short blond hair sitting cross-legged on a bed in a motel room, writing carefully in a Bible—and he blinked.

"At most. She might've still been seven. Three years ago was just when the salesman happened to find it. Listen," Peter said, "I could use your help on this. It's a solvable case, but she could be anywhere, literally anywhere tonight, I am out of leads, and I'm having a bad month. You know Anya left me. Take a leave of absence from the police force, come work with me on this. The money's better."

"Christ, I didn't know about Anya. I'm sorry."

"Well, she always said she was going to. Has it been that long since we've spoken?"

"I guess it's been a while," Christopher said.

"Think about coming to work with me on this. If anyone can find her . . ."

"I'll think about it. May I borrow this?"

"Of course."

He left the bar not long afterward. It was August in Montreal, and an airless day had turned to a perfect evening; there was a cool breeze from the distant river and Rue St.-Denis was alight, outdoor cafés spilling their light and voices out into the street, streetlamps shining down through the leaves of the trees that lined the sidewalk, and people everywhere: couples out walking in the twilight, girls with short skirts and multicoloured hair and combat boots, young men with berets and goatees smoking cigarettes and walking somewhere quickly, slow-moving hippies with scarves wrapped over their dreadlocks, people eating dinner at small round tables on the sidewalk, everyone surreptitiously watching everyone else.

He walked slowly down the long slope to Rue Sainte-Catherine, in love with the city, the Bible in his shoulder bag. It was a lightweight book, mass-produced on thin paper, but he felt the weight. He'd spent his childhood travelling too, and felt a certain empathy on that front, but it seemed to him later that he'd been seduced by her language. *I wish to remain vanishing.* He knew exactly what she meant. He walked home from the jazz club because the walk took two hours and he wanted to be alone, turning the phrase over and over like a polished stone in his pocket. He told himself as he walked that he was trying to make the decision, but realized long before he got home that the decision had already been made.

His wife was in the kitchen, listening to the radio with the newspaper spread out over the table; she looked up and smiled when he looked in but had nothing to say. He smiled back at her and went to the dining room, flicked on the overhead light, opened the Bible on the table to read the note again. He felt less than tranquil. *I do not want to be found.* Later he went upstairs but he couldn't sleep. He got up once to look in on his daughter, asleep under a quilt that had sheep all around the edges. Afterward he lay reading for a long time, an old copy of *Bullfinch's Mythology* that he'd picked up from a street vendor, listening to his wife moving restlessly around the house and turning the radio on and off in the kitchen. Something was bothering him. He put the book down on the bedside table and picked up the Bible again. The child's handwriting obscured part of the Twenty-second Psalm. He read the psalm aloud once, and then recited the first two stanzas by memory to the plaster ceiling: *"Why art thou so far from helping me, and from the words of my roaring? O my God, I cry in the day time, but thou hearest not; and in the night season, and am not silent."*

He heard his wife turn up the volume of the radio somewhere far away in the house, as if she was hoping to drown him out, but realized that she couldn't possibly have heard him. The radio was abstract from this distance, soft static and inaudible voices. He glanced at the bedside clock. It was three-forty-five in the morning.

"If you don't want to be rescued," Christopher said aloud to the ceiling, "then why the Twenty-second Psalm?"

11

On Lilia's twelfth birthday, her father gave her a book of photographs: *Life* magazine's collection of the most memorable images of the twentieth century. Women in bell-bottoms and big round glasses, anti-war banners above a sea of faces on the Washington Mall, cars full of families moving slowly across a 1930s field of dust. But there was a particular image that she turned to over and over again: the crater formed by the Trinity bomb test in the New Mexico desert, in the final year of the Second World War. ("Not far from here," her father said, glancing briefly over her shoulder and then back at the road. "No, we can't visit it. It's still radioactive.")

The crater showed the aftermath of an ungodly heat: the centre was purest black, the brightest black imaginable, and around the edges of this brilliant darkness was a shining ring. This was where the heat of the explosion had changed the sand to glass, and the glass reflected the sky. The same force levels cities and creates mirrors in the desert. It occurred to her that this was what being caught might be like. The white-hot flash of recognition and then her life blown open, a radioactive mirror in a wasteland, her secretive life torn asunder and scattered outward in disarray. Tears came to her eyes in the passenger seat.

"Lilia, Lilia. Let's stop driving for the day. Look, there's a restaurant. Let's get you something to eat . . ."

"Why aren't there any pictures of me?" she asked later, sipping iced tea in the air-conditioned calm of a diner.

"What do you mean?"

"Don't most people have pictures? Of when they were kids?"

He looked at her for a moment and then stood up from

the table. When she looked up he was leaning on the counter, talking to the waitress. He said something that made the waitress laugh and beckoned Lilia over.

"We're in luck, Katie. They do have a camera here."

"So what're you doing travelling on your birthday, Katie?" the waitress asked. She had a cloud of blond curls and red lipstick, and she winked at Lilia while she handed the camera to her father. He motioned Lilia up on a stool and stood back.

"We're going to visit my cousins," Lilia said.

The waitress leaned on the counter to be in the picture, although she hadn't been asked. *Click.* "Much obliged," Lilia's father said. He handed Lilia the Polaroid, and she watched her face rise slowly out of milky white.

Eleven years later she knelt on Eli's bed in Brooklyn and pinned the picture to the wall with a thumbtack.

12

Late at night Christopher liked to read Shakespeare some-times, while he waited for his wife to come to bed or for sleep to overtake him, whichever happened first, and at three in the morning on an unremarkable night he caught himself reading and rereading a line from *Romeo and Juliet*: *My child is yet a stranger in the world.* He had met Peter in the bar only two or three nights earlier, and the line resonated strangely. There was a song playing on the radio a lot around that time with a lyric that he liked, something about being a stranger in your own hometown, and he caught himself singing this line sometimes at quiet moments. His voice was unfamiliar. He'd never sung in his life, except under his breath at birth-day parties, but these days he no longer entirely recognized himself.

Christopher was forty-five that year and felt somewhat older, but on the drive to work this morning he felt younger than he had in years. The Bible with the note from the missing child was in his bag on the passenger side. He hadn't slept much—his wife had taken to coming to bed just before dawn lately, and she talked incoherently in her sleep—but he wasn't tired, and he felt an enormous weight lift from his shoulders when his leave-of-absence request was approved in the early afternoon. A week later he dragged the crate filled with Lilia's case files into a dusty corner office at Peter's agency and began attempting to settle in.

"A change is as good as a vacation," his supervisor had said, a bit too meaningfully in retrospect, when the leave-of-absence request had been granted. This led him to suspect that he'd been becoming a stranger for longer than he realized, perhaps slipping a little in general. He knew he was getting too tired these days, not as self-sustaining as he had been, and his hair was going grey above his ears. He told himself, sitting in the new office that afternoon, that this change was exactly what he needed. He put Michaela's most recent school photograph in a desk drawer, spent a meditative few minutes arranging his notebooks and pens, pulled the first file from the crate, and began to immerse himself in the case. Like sliding into a lake.

There were stills from a surveillance tape in a motel lobby in Cincinnati, the day before Lilia had almost been caught. This would have been two or three years after she'd written in the Bible. Lilia was rendered as a small child with short blond hair, caught at the instant she glanced up into the camera lens. The whole scene was a little fuzzy and unclear in the enlargement, the expression unreadable on her pixilated face. The man behind her could have been anyone: head down, shuffling through a wallet. Notes in Peter's handwriting in the lower margin: *Appears at ease, but he never looks up at cameras.* Christopher flipped back through the folders, feeling less displaced than he'd felt in months, and began reading from the beginning. It began with a missing-persons report, filed in the middle of November some years ago: in a rural area between the small city of Saint-Jean-sur-Richelieu and the American border, a seven-year-old girl disappeared in the night. Her footprints were visible in the snow by the front door. She ran out barefoot onto the lawn, and then someone lifted her and carried her away. The prints of a man's boots led to the tire tracks down by the road.

Sunlight slanted in through the window and warmed the back of Christopher's head. He realized that the angle of light had changed. He was hungry. He'd been reading for hours. The initial investigation seemed somehow botched to him. He had been reading a transcript of an interview with the girl's mother and thinking that she seemed curiously detached, although it was of course a possibility that she had still been in shock at that point. He decided it might be necessary to interview her again at some point. Perhaps Lilia's half-brother as well. He pencilled Lilia's half-brother's name into a notebook, feeling more purposeful than he had in some time.

Christopher rose, stretched, and went out into the street. The air outside was hot and still. Tourists wandered, speaking English in a sea of French. A pair of girls were playing cellos on a street corner, and on the way back to the office with a sandwich and a coffee he stopped to listen to them for a few minutes, sipping his coffee and feeling that everything would be all right. He thought he might speak to his daughter tonight. It had been a long time since he'd had a real conversation with her. He'd ask her about school, maybe even offer to help out with her homework. He'd tell his wife that her hair looked beautiful. Once back at the desk he stretched out his legs and leaned back in the chair, the coffee immediately forgotten on a pile of old notes. He had read through everything. There was a map that Peter had started—a continental road map, four or five possible sightings circled in red with notations. There was a page of typed contact information: Lilia's mother, one of Lilia's schoolteachers, the detective who had initially handled the case.

"You can't," Peter said when Christopher came to him later. "It's in the contract."

"It's in the contract that I can't talk to Lilia's brother? Are you serious?"

"I am. I'm afraid the mother was adamant." Peter was leaning back in his chair with his feet up on his desk, looking through a stack of black-and-white photographs. All twenty of them had been taken within a space of seconds and depicted a man and a woman entering a motel.

"I see."

"Oh, don't read into it," Peter said. "She said her son had been through enough already. I take it the kid's been interviewed repeatedly by the local cops, and I had to agree not to try to speak with him if I was going to take the case. She's just being protective."

"You're certain that you couldn't convince her otherwise?"

"I'm certain. You haven't met this woman."

"Fine."

Christopher returned to his office and closed the door behind him. He spread the map over his desk. He stared at the lines of highways leading out of Cincinnati and let his mind drift, looking for a pattern in the circles and notations and interstate lines, waiting for the old instinct to tell him which way they had gone. He closed his eyes. Follow the trajectory, cities circled in red, a car moving quickly over the surface of a map. His hand was writing her name in the margin of his notebook. *Lilia. Lilia. Lilia. Lilia.* His focus was absolute.

A thousand miles away in another country, but separated from him only by the thinnest possible sheen, a car moved quickly across the New Mexico desert. A landscape composed of sand and light, and the map folded on the dashboard was beginning to fade in the sunlight.

13

There was a red pencil that Lilia's father had purchased specifically for drawing squiggly lines on maps, and in a series of motel rooms they charted a course. They could go almost anywhere. Every direction was possible. They tossed a coin whenever they couldn't reach an immediate agreement—if it's heads we go to Santa Barbara, tails means we're going north—unless there was a music festival or a concert of some sort that her father wanted to go to, in which case he had veto power. In the impeccable past before the broken-down present, in the long hectic interlude before she'd begun leaving people behind, pre-Eli, it sometimes really was as simple as a coin toss.

"One thing you might want to think about," her father said when she was sixteen, "is whether you maybe want to stop travelling someday." She knew him well enough to understand that what he meant was *I'm worried about you, I want you to stop*, but she couldn't. At sixteen she was travelling alone to San Diego, with her father worrying about her in the small town where he'd settled in the New Mexico desert, and when she was seventeen and eighteen she hadn't come back yet, except for short visits, and she passed through another ten or fifteen cities and towns in the confused interlude of time between her eighteenth and twentieth birthdays.

She never asked for money from her father, although he sent it sometimes unsolicited. It was possible to get by, from city to city. There was always a room she could rent, there was always a dishwashing job or a job in a stockroom or a job sweeping the floor in a salon, there was always enough to live on, just barely, and eventually enough to travel away again.

What she aspired to was a kind of delirious perfection. What Lilia wanted was to travel, but not only that; she wanted to be a citizen of everywhere, free-wheeling and capable of instant flight. There were complicated sequences of travel: maps, suitcases, buses moving slowly through the interstate nights, garbled announcements of departures and delays in the tiled aquarium acoustics of train stations, clocks set high on the walls of station waiting rooms.

In San Diego there was no one; she arrived young and exuberantly alone and stayed for three months working in a doughnut shop, and then began making her way up the coast. When she'd reached the top of the American coastline (it seemed unwise to cross the border) she turned and started to make her way back down, and by then she was seventeen and people had begun to attach themselves to her in almost every city she stopped in. In San Francisco there was Edwin. He walked up and down hills in the rain with her and held her hand in the park. In Sacramento there was Arturo, who made exquisite pasta dishes and wanted to be a professional chef. In Santa Paula there was Gene, and Santos lived in Pinto Beach. In Los Angeles there was Trent, and later another Edwin, who was more interesting than the first one but not as kind. Her second time through San Diego there was Gareth, and then she turned inland toward the middle of the continent and a string of barely memorable Michaels and Daves. In her memories of a dozen other cities there are ghosts with no names; conversely, there are several minor lovers whose geographical locations can't be pinpointed in memory beyond small details like a Persian rug in one of their apartments, an angle of streetlight across the living room ceiling of another, a bright-blue alarm clock in the bedroom of a third. The first girl, Lucy, lived in Denver. In Indianapolis there was Peter, who played Vivaldi on his record player and made origami swans. In St. Paul there was a more important Michael, who liked expensive red wine and was trying to be a freelance writer, and in Minneapolis there was Theo. In St. Louis there was no one, but she was only there for a week.

In Chicago there was Erica. Lilia was twenty-two years old by then, getting a little tired and beginning to think about New York, which was one of the few cities in the United States where she had never been. She stayed in Chicago for two months and left with very little warning. On the last night she got into an argument with Erica, and they sat together in silence for a long time afterward at a table by the railing on the high mezzanine of Erica's favourite bar. Erica sipped her beer and gazed down over the edge. It was close to midnight, and a waitress had brought a candle to each table; the candles flickered individually in the dimness and Lilia stared blankly at the hundred scattered bits of flame, thinking of what New York City might be like and how she might get out of the bar without making Erica cry again.

Erica moved her glass in front of the candle. The flame shining through it transformed her beer into a glass of pure light. It took a moment for Lilia to realize that Erica was speaking to her.

"I'm sorry. What were you saying?"

"That waitress," Erica said. "I was saying she's interesting, don't you think?" She was looking down over the mezzanine railing. The girl who'd brought the beer and the candlelight was wiping down a table by the bar, and to Lilia's eye she wasn't fascinating at first glance: white shirt, black pants, well-executed ponytail, autopilot expression, red lipstick.

"What's interesting about her?" Lilia was distracted and upset, thinking of tomorrow morning's bus schedule and never seeing Erica again, and from the mezzanine the waitress just looked like any other waitress. One thing that had begun to trouble Lilia lately was the way that sometimes all people and all cities looked the same to her.

"She has a tattoo on the back of her wrist," said Erica dreamily. "You can see it when she reaches for things." She was watching the girl wipe the surface of a dark wood table.

"So?"

"I like waitresses with tattoos," Erica said. "It implies the existence of a secret life."

Lilia liked this idea, although she didn't tell Erica that, and she saw what Erica meant when the waitress brought a new ashtray. The tattoo was a snake biting its own tail, in a perfect bluish-green infinite circle on the back of her left wrist.

"It's a good tattoo," Lilia said, but Erica's thoughts were already elsewhere. She was smiling at Lilia now, looking at her consideringly. She pushed a long strand of blue hair back from her face before she spoke.

"I still think it's courageous, Lilia," she said brightly, picking up the scent of the earlier argument, "whatever *you* want to call it."

Lilia sighed and sipped half-heartedly at her wine, wishing she was gone already. She had decided earlier in the evening never to give anyone advance warning of departure ever again.

"I mean, I know you *think* it's nothing, but it just impresses me. I could never do that. Just pack up and *go* like that, without any warning, or almost none, to just pick up and move your whole life . . ."

"There's nothing very brave about it, actually. I didn't say it was nothing, I just said it isn't courageous."

"Please." Erica was momentarily distracted by her pint of beer. "Do you even know anyone in New York City?"

Lilia shook her head. She was playing idly with two empty cigarette boxes, combining them with the salt and pepper shakers to build an unstable little house.

"Do you have a place to stay?"

"No."

"A job?"

"I'll find something."

"There, you see?" Erica leaned back in her chair as if she'd just proved something. Her smile bordered on smug. "*That's* courage," she said, "whatever you want to call it."

"You don't understand." Lilia found at that moment that she had no patience for anything: this city, this street, this relentlessly trendy split-level bar, the identically dressed waitresses gliding between tables, this blue-haired girl across the table with the beer. The sadness of the waitress's blue-green snake tattoo, circling forever on the same tired wrist. She let her cigarette-box house fall down in disarray. "It isn't courage, Erica, it's exactly the opposite. There's nothing good about it. It's exactly like running away from everything that matters, and I wish I could make you understand that."

"Please. How many places have you moved to since you went out on your own?"

"Since I was sixteen? I don't know. Maybe twenty. Probably more. But you're still missing the point completely."

"Just in the last two years, say. How many have you moved to in the last two years?"

"I don't know, Erica. You're still not getting this. It's just, listen, I've never moved *to* anywhere in my life. When I show up in a city, it doesn't mean I'm arriving, it only means . . . when I show up," Lilia said, floundering now, repeating herself, "I'm not *arriving* anywhere, I'm only leaving somewhere else."

"I still think—"

"You're not listening. You don't get it. It isn't admirable. I cannot stop. All I ever do is leave, and I apparently don't even do that very well, since you're sitting there starting to cry because I'm leaving tomorrow, and I'm always running out of time. I am always running out of time. This, is all, I ever, do, and there is absolutely nothing admirable about it."

Erica was stricken. The tears were starting to win. This only made her more beautiful, and Lilia thought she might die if the moment didn't end, so she stood up and moved around the table and kissed the blue hair that she'd already kissed so many times. The kiss released a sob, and Erica held one hand over her eyes, her face shining in the candlelight. Lilia was moving quickly past her, down the stairs and out onto the sidewalk, where the Friday-night crowd moved around her like ghosts. She fumbled in her jacket pocket for her cell phone and dialed as she walked down the crowded sidewalk, crossed the street quickly and stood in a doorway while the call went through.

"It's good to hear your voice," her father said. There was a baby crying in the background, her most recent half-sibling, and she could hear his girlfriend's soothing voice. The sounds brought her back to his house in the desert, the smell of french fries in the diner where her father's girlfriend worked, long walks down cracked streets in the cool desert twilight, and she closed her eyes against the sheer oppositeness of the cold bright city. "Where are you?" he asked.

"Still in Chicago." She forced her voice to be light. "But I wanted to call and tell you that I'm moving to New York City tomorrow."

"New York New York," he said. "Fine choice, kiddo. I spent some years there. Do you need money?"

"I'll find another job."

"I'll send you a wire transfer tomorrow."

Across the street, some distance down the block, Erica had emerged from the bar. She had an unsteady look about her. She stood on the edge of the sidewalk, looking up and down the street. Lilia sank back into the doorway.

"Do you know what's strange?" she asked.

"What's that, my dove?"

"I thought I saw the detective in St. Louis a couple of months ago. I walked out of a deli, and there was a man across the street with that same kind of hat, that fedora thing. He had a cane. He was just stepping into another store, and I couldn't see his face, but I felt like he was watching me, just for that instant when I came out of the deli."

"Is that why you left St. Louis?"

"I don't know. Maybe. I wanted to see Chicago again."

"Seems impossible that he'd be around, after what happened," her father said carefully. "Doesn't it?"

"Yeah." Lilia was looking up and down the street, but Erica was nowhere. "It must have been someone else. But it seemed like he was watching me."

"I'm worried about you," her father said.

"Don't be. I'm always fine."

"I know you're always fine," he said, "but there's no reason to be travelling quite so constantly these days, wouldn't you agree?"

"You taught me how to travel."

"Quite true, my lily. However, since you were so clearly paying attention to my example, you'll notice that I did eventually stop. Have you considered settling somewhere for a year or two, just as an experiment?"

"The thought does cross my mind occasionally."

"No one's watching you anymore."

"How can you be sure?"

"Because you're not an abducted child, you're a legal adult. No one has any reason to be looking for you. You successfully disappeared."

"A private detective could still look for me."

"He was in an accident," her father said softly.

"He was from Montreal, wasn't he? It made me want to go there. Just to finally face it."

"Of all places," said her father. "Don't."

14

There was a cufflink under the bed when Christopher reached down for his slippers that morning. *That* morning, the morning he'd always remember, a few months after he'd taken Lilia's case. He picked it up with the care of a jeweller handling a diamond, examined it from every angle, held it to the light. It was unextraordinary. It also wasn't his. His wife lay sleeping at the far edge of the bed, close against the wall. Christopher dressed slowly and put the cufflink in his pocket. He felt that the right thing to do in these circumstances would be to wake her, either to ask her or just to hold it up in silence until she said something, wept, denied, confessed, but his thoughts were scattered, he couldn't bring himself to do it, and he realized as he watched her sleep that he was thinking of lions. Of chasing his future wife down the midway when they were eleven and ten, of travelling with her across the length of nine provinces and thirty-four states, over the border and back again. He ran two red lights by accident on his way to work that morning.

The cufflink was composed of two plastic buttons with a bit of wire between them, obviously from a very cheap shirt. He sat at his desk, turning it over and over between his fingers. A salesman? Door-to-door? Vacuum cleaners? Insurance? Days had passed now since he'd found it, and he'd hardly been home. His wife hadn't commented. She was working longer hours herself, and she'd been unusually courteous of late. Polite strangers in the bedroom. They barely spoke. But he still imagined, watching her sleep at night, that all of this might still be salvageable in some way. He sometimes touched her pale hair on the pillow and imagined what he might say to her if he had the strength of will to say it. He felt that he was working his way up to something, an action of some kind, some redemptive collection of words that would restore his marriage and bring her back to him and make Michaela reachable again, all at once. It wasn't impossible. He began a separate set of notes, somewhat random, unrelated to Lilia's case. Notes on the second law of thermodynamics, memorized in high school: *The second law of thermodynamics states that all systems tend toward entropy. Is this irreparable, or might the process be reversed?* Notes on Michaela: *skittish, secretive, brown hair, green eyes.* Notes on his wife: *governed inordinately by the second law of thermodynamics.* Christopher was careful to keep this notebook separate from the other ones and leave it at the office. He labelled it *Family* and put it in a drawer. He read through these notes sometimes when it was late and he'd been working all day and he couldn't read one more word or make one more phone call about his missing Lilia. *Michaela: always quiet at dinner, can't meet her eyes across the dinner table some nights. The feeling of one's daughter having been replaced by a changeling. Elaine: barely sleeps, but never seems tired. Red garnet earrings. Matching red nails.* He wished to come home one evening and perform a pulling-together motion, like tying a piece of string; he spent a great deal of time thinking about how he might achieve this, and these other notes felt like preparation. At some point, he felt, he'd have amassed enough evidence to have a complete picture of the situation, at which point he could act decisively and pull things back together again.

There were a few days when he felt that the preparations were going smoothly, that he was approaching the level of understanding that he needed, but then there was a tie he didn't recognize on the floor of his closet. He saw it when he was getting dressed one morning, a week or two after the cufflink. It lay discarded, as if thrown carelessly from elsewhere in the room. But the angle didn't work, he'd tried to throw things into the closet often enough to know that it just wasn't possible, things thrown from the room hit the wall or the closet door, even if the closet door happened to be open, ergo, the tie was obviously planted. He was a detective, for God's sake. He knew he was being baited and that he should say something, that he was *meant* to say something and that saying something might even help, but the tie made everything seem foreign and unsalvageable and impossible again. On the way to work he talked to himself, trying to summon something—sadness? anger?—alarmed by a soft but unmistakable sense of relief. At least, he thought, things were becoming clearer. Much later he sat at his desk in the dwindling evening, looking at the cufflink and lost in the past.

He'd met his wife when they were children in a travelling circus. Strange upbringing by most standards, but it had seemed normal at the time: his father was a lion tamer, and her parents walked on tightropes. A childhood played out across a thousand dusty towns between Vancouver and Halifax, in the bright perilous years when most people still took their kids to circuses and everyone was waiting for the atomic bomb to drop and the Soviet Union was still intact, still the dark empire far away across the sea, and Elaine had permanently skinned knees and ribbons in her hair and ferocious arguments with her parents. She hated tightrope walking. She came from a long line of tightrope walkers. Her parents didn't understand why their daughter hated the profession so much, and were somewhat inclined to take it personally. There were winters spent waiting for the season to start, staring out the classroom window at the winter sunlight thinking about leaving again, meeting Elaine in the hallways and counting down the days with her—"Twenty-six days," she'd say mysteriously, as she passed, and the other kids around them pretended not to be envious because everyone wants to travel away with a circus, "Fifteen days," "Four," until finally she could whisper "Tomorrow," with her eyes all alight, because even if she didn't want to be a tightrope walker, the thought of going to school for longer than a semester at a time seemed unbearably stultifying to both of them; and then in the very early morning, the long caravan of transport trucks moving east out of Calgary while he lay on the floor of their moving house and read Spiderman comics. Elaine, his best and only friend, sometimes travelled in his family's trailer with him between stops. He kissed her for the first time between Toronto and Ottawa.

Decades later in Montreal, Christopher closed his eyes, his fist clenched over the cufflink, rested his elbows on his desk and his forehead on his fists. He remained that way for several minutes, unmoving, and then straightened very slowly, placed the cufflink in the drawer that held Michaela's school picture, and reached for the stack of files on the edge of his desk. He opened the top folder, and unfolded a map with Lilia's name written twenty-eight times in the margin. He was aware that he'd been neglecting his other cases.

He followed her quietly over the mountains, tracing lines on maps of the North American continent, making phone calls, talking to far-off police departments, picking up sightings, rumours, tips. He followed her out of his life and into a hinterland composed of folders and documents, each holding the keys to her missing life, his path through the wilderness marked by coffee rings. He worked late into the night. By now there were over a hundred pages of documents relating to the case: photographs, police reports, possible sightings. Memory reduced to manila envelopes and typed documents, stills from surveillance videos, early-childhood photographs. There was one photograph in particular that haunted him. It had been used by the local press shortly after her disappearance, and it depicted two unsmiling dark-haired children, Lilia and her half-brother Simon, in front of their beaming mother on the steps of a distant porch. The small boy has his arm around his tiny sister. The two children gaze seriously at the camera, their mother radiant behind them. What drives a seven-year-old to run out barefoot into snow? The question troubled him.

Still, Lilia wasn't far away from him. As the months passed he felt at times that he was getting close. There were strange moments like flashes of light, when he looked at the map and thought he knew where she was. The old intuition that had sometimes unnerved his colleagues in the police department. He brought the folders home in the evenings and spread documents over the dining room table. From there he followed the missing girl over the desert, like something winged and distant in the blazing sky. The car sped down the highway, just out of sight, while he stared at a map in his dining room in Montreal. Michaela watched his departure from the stairs.

He glanced at his daughter across the dining room table sometimes, on the increasingly rare nights when they all sat down for dinner together, and silently wondered if he would be able to explain this to her later on, in some unimaginably pleasant future when they could sit down for a drink together, just the two of them, reconciled in Michaela's adulthood: I wasn't avoiding you, it wasn't your fault, but there was a cufflink and a tie and she wasn't speaking to me, and my marriage . . . The explanation fell apart even in his mind. (Notes on the second law of thermodynamics: *All systems tend inevitably toward entropy. Why should my family be any exception?*)

15

When Lilia was very young the entire world seemed composed of motel rooms, strung like an archipelago across the continental United States. Island life was fast and transient, all cars and motel rooms and roadside diners, trading used cars at sketchy neighbourhoods, long rides down highways in the sunlight, in the rain, talking to waitresses who thought she was too young for coffee, nights spent under the scratchy sheets of cheap roadside motels, messages written secretly in motel-room Bibles. *I don't want to be found.*

There were hours spent in quiet libraries. Her father brought her history books, books about science, books about people he thought she should be aware of, then sat nearby reading the paper while she worked her way through the stack. He tested her on comprehension back in the motel room in the evening. There were sometimes questions: "Isn't it a school day?" a librarian or a bookstore clerk would ask.

Her father had coached her in the appropriate response: "I'm home-schooled," Lilia said. If this seemed insufficient, she added, "for religious reasons." She liked books, but the hours spent in small-town libraries were tedious, and she began the first list when she was eight or nine as a means of distraction. A list of names, eventually expanding to ten or twelve pages: Lilia, Gabriel, Anna, Michelle. In every town her name was different; there were often, especially in the beginning, several names and stories in the course of any given month. At first Lilia and her father concocted the stories carefully together and practised them on the way into town. Later they could play off each other without rehearsal—"Elizabeth," he'd call out, in the magazine section of a gas station store (those bright new stores, too large for the smallness of the town outside, with rows of shiny packaging and a strange stale smell like dead coffee and mildew), "Elizabeth, it's time to go—" and although she wouldn't ever have been called that name before, she'd recognize his voice and turn around and smile just like a real Elizabeth would, and then note the new name on the list in a library later. It wasn't an unhappy life. She liked travelling.

But the sense of being chased overtook him without warning. It always registered first as a tension in his hands on the steering wheel. He would start tapping out a rhythm on the wheel with his thumb and two fingers, a beating three-four rhythm, fast ruinous waltz. Sometimes he glanced in the rear-view mirror and thought he saw something, or saw nothing but was frightened anyway, and he motioned silently toward the backseat. She would climb between the front seats and slip into the back of the car, frightened into smallness, and hide in a private improvised tent.

In the first year her father used to pull the car over and hide her, but later she knew how to build her own shelter, and she'd perfected her hiding place by the time she turned eight. She knew how to build a tent with blankets and pillows and suitcases in the backseat of a car, a way of disappearing into the chaos of luggage and pillows and blankets and coats. She hid there by the hour in the shifting darkness until her clothes clung to her body with sweat. She was suspicious of the dark, so her father gave her a flashlight, and she liked to shine it in circles on the blanket ceiling, practising a new kind of cursive writing, drawn in light, and the car moved beneath her like a ship. She pretended she was a stowaway crossing hazardous seas. A fugitive, always. When she was small she imagined that her tent was dug deep into snow far up in the Arctic, or half buried in a sandstorm in a hot treacherous land. She imagined there were search parties out looking for her—Bedouin nomads, explorers on sleighs drawn by teams of huskies, sailors going through the crates and spools of rope in the depths of the ship—but in her happiest daydreams they passed her by. She was never unearthed from the snowdrift, the nomads never found her in the sand dunes, she was never pulled flailing up out of the hold. She lay still by the hour, lost and undiscovered, and she sometimes imagined Simon lying there beside her, although the details of his face were fading and she wasn't sure she remembered what he looked like anymore, and the beam of her flashlight traced patterns on the blanket overhead. The light circling like a signal in her limited sky.

16

When Michaela was eleven and twelve and thirteen she liked movies about cat burglars, and had ideas about dynamite. It wasn't so much a yearning to blow up anything specific, it was more a notion that she could probably figure out how to make things explode if she had to. She had similar suspicions about scaling the walls of bank towers and walking on tight-ropes across streets, but her feelings about tightropes were much more definite, or at the very least better-informed: partly on the theory that talent skips generations and partly to appease two sets of disappointed grandparents, it had been decided very early on to send Michaela to circus school. Three days a week after school she took a bus to a neigh-bourhood near McGill University, arriving early if at all possible. The circus school, a dusty venture run out of a vaulted church basement by double-jointed Moscow Circus veterans, was equipped with a rudimentary high wire, and she spent as much time as possible walking back and forth.

At home she had a practice tightrope installed in the living room. It was only a foot off the floor but she imagined a hundred feet of space beneath her, crowds cheering, all the people and lights. Or absolute stillness between bank towers, making a perfect getaway with the safety-deposit-box master key, moving like water over the opposite window ledge. She walked back and forth, back and forth, expert and alone. The tightrope walking calmed her when the house was too silent and no one else was home. It seemed that the length of time between the end of school and her parents' return home was growing longer from one evening to the next. Michaela felt herself to be on the vanguard of a brave new world. It was as if her parents had simply given her the house. Her father came home late and had little to say. He spread his files over the dining room table after dinner and stayed there poring over them deep into the night. He stood sometimes, he paced, he threw back his head and closed his eyes, he said a name sometimes aloud like a mantra (*Lilia, Lilia*), but he never looked up and saw his daughter watching through the banister railings. There were nights when she fell asleep on the stairs.

Her mother came home around midnight, and carried the child up to bed. She kissed her softly on the forehead and Michaela opened her eyes for a moment, not quite awake: *Why do you work so much?* Sometimes her mother didn't answer. Sometimes she did: *Because I have things to do, my darling. Everyone around here is consumed by work, haven't you noticed?* She held Michaela close against her, and the collar of her blouse smelled faintly of tobacco and aftershave.

"*I FIND HER* somewhat . . . ferocious," the seventh-grade teacher said diplomatically, in the last parent-teacher conference Michaela's mother ever attended.

"Really," said Michaela's mother. She was interested but having a hard time concentrating. "Ferocious?"

"*Intense,*" said the teacher immediately, attempting to switch the words in mid-air. "She's very focused. Ms. Graydon, I think we need to discuss your daughter's progress in French."

This was a matter of lingering concern among the faculty. Michaela had qualified for a coveted English-language education under the terms of Quebec's language laws, and had been failing her French classes since the first grade.

"Oh, I imagine she'll pick it up," said Michaela's mother. She was running her fingers through her hair and looking down at the floor. "I should get back to the office," she announced abruptly. "My boss is waiting for me."

"Of course," said Michaela's teacher. "I just think—"

"That she's ferocious?"

"I was going to say, I just think that we may be looking at dyslexia at this point. Her grades are excellent in every subject except French. She just doesn't seem able to pick it up. I don't have to tell you that in this political climate, an inability to speak the language—"

"Ferocious," Michaela's mother persisted, smiling slightly.

"A little, well, a little intense. Yes." The teacher couldn't help but notice that Michaela's mother seemed almost pleased by this. It wasn't so disturbing that she ever mentioned it to anyone, but she didn't schedule any more meetings with Michaela's parents.

The following week Christopher received a call from the circus school—Michaela, a young assistant informed him breathlessly, had fallen off the high wire—his breath caught in his throat—but she'd only sprained her ankle, all was well, could he come and pick her up? Michaela's mother, inexplicably, couldn't be reached. Michaela didn't tell anyone that she'd hardly seen her father in two weeks. He stood awkwardly in the church basement with his hands in his coat pockets, gloomy about the interruption from his work but too conscious of appearances not to show up, and examined her ankle along with her instructor. He agreed that it was slightly swollen and that she'd probably be fine by tomorrow.

"How did you fall off a high wire?" he asked. "There's supposed to be a safety net."

"I sprained my ankle in the safety net," she said. "It was the safety net that distracted me and made me fall in the first place."

"How can a safety net distract you?"

"It moved," she said. "Someone brushed up against it from underneath. If it hadn't been there, I probably would've been fine."

"If it hadn't been there—" her father said, but then found

that he couldn't finish the sentence. He cleared his throat.

"Well," her instructor said. He was a middle-aged man with a Russian accent and a missing finger on his left hand. "You'll want to take her home, I imagine."

"Yes," Christopher said, surprised by the notion. "Yes, of course. Thank you." He nodded awkwardly and walked with his daughter out into the street. This was one of the neighbourhoods that he loved the most, and he was thinking about how rarely he came up here. The architecture was beautiful in this corner of town. They walked together for a few minutes in silence, Michaela limping, Christopher looking at the spiral staircases on the outside of the buildings.

"Dad?" He looked at her, startled out of his thoughts, but wasn't sure what to say. "Dad, I want to join the circus."

"Absolutely not," he said.

"Why not?" she asked, a little petulant. She increased the severity of her limp for a few steps.

"You can't join a circus," he said. "You're thirteen."

"Fourteen. There's a girl a year older than me at the circus school who already worked with Cirque du Soleil when she was my age. I could audition," she said.

He decided to ignore this. "Tightrope walking is not a life," he said. "And besides your age, you know why not. It's devolution." The thought of joining circuses upset him. He'd run away from his parents' circus with his wife when they were seventeen and eighteen.

"What's devolution?"

"The opposite of evolving. Why would you want to join a circus?"

"To travel away," Michaela said. "I don't like it here."

"Sure you do."

"I *don't*. I can't even speak French," she said, "and *everyone* speaks French. Why can't I move somewhere else and join a circus?"

"Because," he said, "you should be happy here. Do you have any idea how difficult it was to get you into an English school? And now you want to speak *French?*" He was hailing a cab. When one pulled up he gave his address, his daughter, and a ten-dollar bill to the cab driver and saw them off with a wave. He was thinking about Lilia. The cab glided to a halt in front of the house, and Michaela gave the ten to the driver, who said something she didn't understand in French. She climbed awkwardly out of the cab, ignoring him, and limped to the front door while the cab pulled away. Her ankle hurt. She unlocked the door and relocked it behind her. The house was silent. There was a dusty umbrella near her feet. She kicked it, limped a few steps toward the stairs, changed her mind and went to the dining room instead. She stopped just inside, went back out to the hall closet, and groped around on the top shelf until she found the in-case-of-emergency flashlight.

The first notebook that she opened began with the chambermaid. Michaela played the flashlight over the page. She could have just turned on the dining room light, but she was pretending to be a cat burglar. The notebook began with a Motel 6 in the town of Leonard, Arizona, a room on the second floor paid for in cash by a man travelling alone with his daughter, a thirty-two-year-old chambermaid's utterly forgettable name. *(Sara? Kate? Jane?)* She squinted (the name was written illegibly) and turned the page.

Lilia was far from Arizona on that particular afternoon. While Michaela was reading those pages in Montreal, she was fly-fishing with her father in an Oregon river. But a year earlier, in a small desert town, Lilia had stayed with her father in a room the chambermaid had cleaned.

17

The room the chambermaid cleaned: two double beds with scratchy orange-and-white-patterned bedspreads, separated by a bedside table containing a motel pen and a Gideon Bible. A TV on a low dresser at the foot of the beds. Lilia's father had gone to get takeout hamburgers at the restaurant downstairs. Lilia was sitting on a bed with a new *National Geographic*, reading about sea horses. The lamps cast a yellowish light, and the television flickered quiet and blue, and the painting on the wall behind her was a splash of abstract colour in the mirror above the television set. Until that night, although never afterward, she always kept the television on for company in the rare times when she was alone in any given room. Lilia was unused to being alone, and the state made her uneasy. She seldom paid attention to the television. On this particular evening she looked up only because she heard her name.

"Lilia Grace Albert," the host intoned. He stood in an industrial-looking multilevel set, where people with their backs to the camera typed on computers. "It's every parent's nightmare," he continued darkly. "A non-custodial parent with citizenship in two nations abducts his daughter, in this case snatching her from her bed in the dead of night, and spirits her away into another country. Once there, it's relatively easy to change her name, to assume a new identity, and, in short, to disappear. Our focus this episode is on the problem of international abductions. We'll examine several individual cases . . ."

It was *Unsolved Cases*, and Lilia was Unsolved that night. Her father's image flashed across the screen, followed by the last school photograph taken before she had disappeared.

The host was talking ponderously about the problem of international abductions in general and Lilia's case in particular, which was apparently considered especially dramatic because of the snatched-from-her-own-bed angle. She was thinking that her picture wasn't bad, as school photographs go. In the first grade she'd been wide-eyed and serious, pretty in an unsmiling way. Her father's photograph, on the other hand, was the photo her mother had supplied to the police shortly after Lilia vanished. The photo had been taken fourteen years earlier at an airport in Nairobi, on the way home from a disastrous African honeymoon: Lilia's father leaned on a concrete pillar near baggage claim, wild-eyed with malarial fever, his hair sticking up in all directions and three days' beard on his face. He looked exactly like the kind of man who'd snatch a child from her bed.

Cut to the face of a pretty young interviewer, all impeccable makeup and perfect hair. She sat on an armchair angled toward a sofa, on which a woman identified in subtitles as Lilia's mother was sitting beside Lilia's brother, who was awkward in a transitional teenaged way and didn't look much like Lilia at all. In the dim light of the motel room Lilia studied them, but their faces stirred nothing in her. They were utterly unfamiliar. She had no recollection of ever having seen them before. The time before she left her mother's house was all closed doors and blind corners; her memories began the night her father appeared on the lawn below her window.

"It's been a difficult few years for you," the interviewer remarked. Her suit was the colour of roses.

"Very difficult," Lilia's mother said. It seemed to Lilia that she had once been very pretty, but now she had a benign, faded look, tired and a little worn. She wore a very large turquoise pendant over a big grey sweater. Her hair looked a little like Lilia's, or the way Lilia thought her hair would look if she stopped dyeing it a different colour every three months. In that moment, sitting on the motel-room bed, Lilia would have given almost anything to remember her mother. The woman on the screen could have been anyone.

"Have there been any recent developments in the case?"

"I've recently engaged the services of a private investigative agency." She spoke with a slight accent that Lilia couldn't quite place.

"A private detective."

"A private detective, yes. It does make me feel that things are hopeful, although of course it's all been very difficult. And there have actually been a few promising leads recently, since the agency began working for me. They're working with the FBI. I think it's hopeful."

"I'm so glad. What has been the most difficult aspect for you," the interviewer asked, "on a day-to-day basis?" She leaned a hairbreadth closer, all warmth and concern and hoping-for-higher-ratings harmlessness, and the camera closed in on the mother's face.

"The nights are difficult. When I sleep," and her mother's voice was strained, "I sometimes dream that she's leaving me. She was so *little*, she was only seven that year, and I always dream of her walking away down the stairs . . ."

She trailed off. The camera tried to catch Lilia's brother, but he was staring uncooperatively into space. He seemed, if anything, beside himself with boredom.

"Would you like a tissue?" the interviewer asked rhetorically. A box of tissues had appeared on a small table by the arm of the sofa. Lilia's mother took one and touched it lightly to her eyes, and then her hands folded and refolded it into a tiny white square on her lap.

"She's mine," Lilia's mother said quietly. "She belongs with me."

"Of course she does. Of course. Let's talk about your son

for a moment. Simon no longer lives with you, is that correct?"

"Simon lives with my first husband," her mother said, "but he still comes to stay with me on weekends."

"Simon," the interviewer said, "would you like to talk a little bit about your sister?"

The camera cut to Simon, but he just looked at his shoes.

"What do you find yourself wishing for the most, more than anything else in the world?" the interviewer asked quickly.

"I wish more than anything that she would come home to me. She belongs with her mother. But if she doesn't, if she can't, if something—if she won't come home, then I wish . . ."

The interviewer leaned forward in her armchair, waiting. Simon said something inaudible and looked away, and it was difficult to escape the impression that he'd heard all this before. What was strange to Lilia, staring at the television, was that she thought the words she almost heard from him were French.

"I know it's terrible." Her mother touched the tissue lightly to her eyes. "I mean, it's terrible even to *think* it, but . . ." Lilia touched her hands to her face while her mother kept speaking, saltwater on her fingertips, and the motel room grew dim around her. All she could see was the television screen, while the room around it faded to outlines and shadows. "But the thought of her disappearance is so terrible, I sometimes wish I could forget . . ." She trailed off, twisting the tissue in her hands, and Lilia touched her fingertips to her lips.

"Forget the abduction?" the interviewer asked.

"No. I wish I could forget her."

(Michaela, one year later in another country, rewound the tape to make sure she'd heard right: *No . . . forget her.*)

Lilia knelt by the side table between the beds, extracted the hotel-room Bible from the top drawer and opened it to the Sixty-ninth Psalm, fumbled in the drawer for a motel pen. She wrote fast and scrawling over the text on the page, *I am not missing. Stop searching for me. I want to stay with my father. Stop searching for me. Leave me alone.* She signed her name and her hand was shaking, because there were still people in the world who wanted her found: she had been leaving this message in motel-room Bibles for so long now, so long, and the messages were reaching no one. It was like throwing messages in bottles into the ocean, but the bottles were drifting away from shore. There were still invisible forces moving against her, and now her picture was shining on a million screens. She left the Bible open on the bed and went to her suitcase, where her plastic change purse was a solid weight in the inner pocket. She took it with her when she slipped out of the room.

Outside the air was bright and still. It was night, but the motel balcony was made shadowless by a long line of bare light bulbs, one above every closed blue door. Lilia left the door to the motel room slightly ajar. This was a prearranged signal: it meant that something was wrong and she was waiting in the car. From the motel balcony she surveyed the topography: there was the long low motel, a bright sprawling chain restaurant, and a gas station between them. The buildings formed a rough L shape on a large parking lot. A few trucks were parked off to one side, and some distance beyond them, across the highway and away in the chaparral, the town of Leonard was a scattering of lights. There were two streetlights in the parking lot, and around them a halo of bugs swirled in a frenzy of wings. She could see the pay phone in the shadows by the restaurant, a hundred miles of parking lot away.

She moved as quietly as possible along the balcony, down

the stairs, aware of the weight of every footstep. The stairs were enclosed and lit too brightly, and at every corner she expected the loom of a police officer, the dark uniform, the badge: *Are you Lilia Grace Albert? We just arrested your father. Would you come with us, please?* But she kept moving down the stairs as silently as possible, clutching the change purse and trying to be invisible. She had to leave the shadows along the edge of the motel and run across the harrowing brilliance of the parking lot to get to the pay phone; once there she fell panting into the booth, convinced that everything was lost, and it took several fast heartbeats to realize that no one had seen her, or if they had they didn't care. No heavy hand clamped down on her shoulder, no footsteps rang out on the parking-lot pavement, no sirens cut the dry desert air. Only three or four cars were parked here, and there were only a few silhouettes visible through the bright windows of the restaurant, where a television was shining above the bar. She couldn't see her father among them. Shadows moved here and there behind the curtains of the motel windows, ghosts against the blue flicker of a dozen screens. She turned her back on the motel and lifted the receiver, and what was strange was that she knew the number to dial when she lifted her hand. There was silence, and then a recorded voice asking for three dollars and seventy-five cents made her jump. She fumbled in the change purse and dropped in quarters and nickels and dimes until a robotic *Thank you* sounded; the coins clicked softly and she turned again so that she could watch the parking lot, the dark silhouettes of gas pumps, the ceaseless movement of waitresses behind the windows of the restaurant. The steel phone cord was cool against her arm. A wind had started out of nowhere, and tumbleweeds rolled fast on the dead sand and asphalt just outside the lights of the parking lot, and she stood still, her heart pounding, listening to the sounds of the call going through. There was a click and then another, switches flicking across a continent of miscrossed wires, over oceans of static and disarray.

Someone answered on the second ring. And she'd known exactly what she was going to say as she dialed the number: *I'm not missing, I don't want to be found, tell them to stop looking for me, I want to stay with my father, I will never come back again and I don't want anyone to find me*, the same thing she'd written in a dozen variations in motel-room Bibles across the United States, but it wasn't her mother who answered the phone.

"*Oui?*" Simon's voice was indistinct. There was a whisper of static on the line. *Simon stays with me on weekends.* Lilia realized that it was a Saturday, and also that she couldn't form a sound in her throat.

She stood frozen in the shadows of the phone booth, the receiver pressed hard against her face.

"Is anyone there?" he asked, in French.

The breeze was picking up. A tumbleweed the size of a rabbit was skittering across the parking lot, and she was watching its escape. She was looking at the parking-lot lights, the way they swayed slightly in the wind, the haze of winged specks fluttering around them. Across the parking lot she saw her father moving on the upper balcony, toward the abandoned room. He pushed open the door and the flicker of the television went dark. She couldn't speak. She couldn't put down the phone.

"Who is this?" He was at an age where his voice was breaking; it cracked across two octaves as he spoke.

"Simon." Her voice was hoarse. "*C'est Lilia.*"

"Where are you?" he whispered.

"I'm travelling," she said.

"Lilia," he whispered. "Lilia, don't stop. Don't come home."

Her father was coming out of the motel room now, hurrying the length of the second-floor balcony, jackets over his shoulder, a suitcase in either hand.

"Keep travelling," her brother whispered. "You have to stay away, even if you're in trouble, no matter where you are . . ."

Her father disappeared into the stairwell, almost running, and in that instant she found that she could run too. She let the receiver fall on its cord, the spell broken, running now, and she was across the parking lot before her father reached the foot of the stairs. In those days they were crossing Arizona in a red convertible. She climbed over the door and curled into the passenger seat, gasping, a moment before her father emerged from the stairwell and the suitcases landed in the seat behind her. A second later her father was beside her. He threw the car into reverse and backed out of the parking lot. The car sped lurchingly out onto the highway, and she stared up at streetlights passing against the indigo sky.

He didn't speak for a long time. He was tapping a nervous waltz rhythm on the wheel. His other hand was a steady, reassuring weight on Lilia's shoulder.

"You saw the show, and you went straight to the car," he said. "That was good. I'm proud of you. You did the right thing."

"I can't remember her."

"Well. You were young."

"I can remember my phone number," she said.

"Your phone number? Really?"

"I can remember my phone number from when I was seven, but I can't remember her."

"Memory's a strange thing."

"Can't you tell me anything?"

He was quiet.

"Please."

"You meet a beautiful divorcée in a bar," he said finally. "She's twenty-six years old with a two-year-old son, she's beautiful, she's alive, she wants to go to Africa for your honeymoon, and then it all goes dark so quickly, and the next thing you know you're taking your kid away in the night. She's the past, kiddo. You don't want to live in the past, and I don't want to talk about it."

"What was her accent?"

"What?"

"My mother," she said. "In the interview. She had an accent."

"She's from Quebec," he said after a very long pause. "But I'm surprised you noticed it. Her English is immaculate."

"What was my first language?"

"What?"

"Was it English or French?"

"We lived near Montreal," her father said. "Just north of the American border. Your mother and I spoke both English and French. You always knew both languages."

"But which was my first?"

"There was no *first*," he said. "You have no first language."

"How can someone have no first language?"

"You just always knew both. Your mother was French, and I was English, and it's just the way it was. But it's no good living in the past, my dove. I don't want to talk about this." And then he said, again, "I'm surprised you noticed her accent."

She couldn't speak, freighted by treason. The streetlights became fewer and farther between until they were replaced altogether by stars, achingly close in the dry night air. It took her a few weeks to understand that Simon had told no one. If he had, Lilia realized, she would have been caught that night.

Simon told no one. He'd always known exactly why his sister had gone away.

He hung up the phone, pressed *69, and wrote the number on the palm of his hand. But before that he stayed on the line until Lilia's quarters ran out, listening to static and the desert wind.

The phone records for Lilia's mother's house arrived on Christopher's desk once a month in a thick envelope, and a couple of years after he'd taken the case he could skim through the pages quickly. He knew most of the numbers by heart. The dentist, the psychiatrist, her first husband's house where her son lived most of the time, her son's friends in Saint-Jean-sur-Richelieu when he was visiting her on the weekends—and here he stopped cold at an incoming call from a foreign telephone number. The duration of the call had been a little over five minutes. He dialed the number and listened to the endless ringing. No one picked up. He wrote, *Pay phone?* in the lower margin and within an hour had confirmed his suspicion.

"Only a week," he told his wife that evening. They sat on opposite sides of the bed, formally, like lovers at the calm ending of a motel-room affair.

"A week," she repeated tonelessly. He'd never left her alone before.

"It could be a breakthrough," he said. "I spoke to the girl's mother, and she knew nothing. She said she was out that night. I asked if I might speak to her son, and she reminded me of the terms of her contract and then hung up on me. I think Lilia's brother could easily have spoken to one of them, the girl or her father, but if I can't talk to him, I have to just . . . Listen, you know I hate leaving you alone."

She smiled suddenly, insincerely it seemed to him, and said, "Well. I hope you have a lovely time."

"It's work," he said. "Not a vacation. I'm just going to fly down for a week and rent a car and ask some questions. It's a hell of a long shot."

"Well, try to have a lovely time anyway."

"Thank you," he said awkwardly. "Thank you, I'll try."

In Arizona he stood before the pay phone in the noonday sun. He could almost see her there in front of him, a ghost, a mirage, dialing a number dredged up from some recess of childhood memory. He turned back toward the motel. It was the middle of the afternoon, and the parking lot was silent. Two cars and an eighteen-wheeler shimmered in the heat. He stood facing the motel until he saw what he was looking for: a movement of white on the upstairs balcony, a chambermaid pushing her cart between rooms. He was walking across the expanse of parking lot when she disappeared into a dim open doorway, the door a rectangle of shadow in the brilliant light. He tried to walk loudly on the balcony so she wouldn't be startled by anyone sneaking up behind her, but she still jumped and pressed a hand briefly to her chest when he knocked on the door of the room she was cleaning.

"I apologize for disturbing you," he said. "Christopher Graydon. I'm a private investigator."

She smiled and told him a name that he wrote illegibly in his notebook. The chambermaid had lived all her life in the town of Leonard. In the long hot afternoon after the interview had aired, she had been vacuuming the abandoned room. She'd found the key in the door that morning. She hadn't seen the *Unsolved Cases* episode, but she had noticed the Bible, left open on a bed with a note across the page. She'd read the note a few times, frowning. There was something a little creepy about the note, and she'd suddenly felt like she was being watched and the silence in the room was oppressive, so she'd closed the Bible quickly and put it away in the drawer. She hadn't thought of it again until Christopher appeared in the doorway of a room she was cleaning two weeks later.

"This will sound like a very strange request," he said after he introduced himself, "but I wonder if you might remember . . ."

The chambermaid had always wanted to be famous. And she was, very briefly, in the town where she lived: "Local Tip Brings Breakthrough in Missing Girl Case" (*Leonard Gazette*, issue number 486), and she smiled beneath the caption with resplendently bleached hair and hoop earrings. "I didn't think nothing of it," she told the newspaper reporter, who changed *nothing* to *anything* before the story went to press. "Just that it was kind of weird, you know, to write something in a Bible like that, but then a detective came to see me."

The detective rented a car and spent six weeks driving, tracing wider and wider circles around the town of Leonard, stopping at motels, asking questions, pulling over to close his eyes and try to imagine which way they might have gone. He called Peter, who told him to stay down there as long as he needed to; his other cases could wait. He called his wife on two consecutive evenings but got only the answering machine and so gave up trying to reach her and continued driving. On the flight home from Tempe he held the new Bible open on his lap, his eyes falling back to the message when he wasn't staring out the window. The handwriting was scrawled and uneven. She was writing fast. *I am not missing. Stop searching for me. I want to stay with my father. Stop searching for me. Leave me alone.—Lilia.*

She had written *Stop searching for me* twice. He thought she must have just seen the *Unsolved Cases* episode, or perhaps she'd been watching it as she wrote. He imagined her writing from the edge of panic, her image flashing across the screen. She understood that she was being pursued. Her strain, telegraphed back to him through this latest message, seemed to Christopher like an acknowledgement of his existence; after two years of pursuit she had received the message that he was following her, opened a Bible to the Sixty-ninth Psalm, and written a reply. He imagined that she was speaking to him. He arrived back in Montreal in the early afternoon, and went directly from the airport to the office instead of going home. He stared at the photograph in her file, the first-grade school portrait that had been used on *Unsolved Cases*, and caught himself whispering the same words over and over again, looking into her inscrutable eyes: *Where do you go? Where do you go?* He felt he'd never been so close.

MICHAELA'S MOTHER began smoking in her husband's absence but neglected to purchase ashtrays. When Christopher came home there was a burnt smell in the air, and there were cigarette burns here and there on the furniture. He would have thought himself to be the kind of man who draws the line somewhere, but he found it no easier to talk to her about putting out cigarettes on the furniture than about strange ties and cufflinks. He purchased a number of cheap glass ashtrays and left them here and there throughout the house. He began going to the office before sunrise, and he didn't come home before dark. He slept with his secretary occasionally, but his heart wasn't really in it. Michaela carefully collected perfect grades, attended the circus school in the afternoons, and began walking home from the bus stop as slowly as she possibly could.

Michaela's mother was losing interest in domesticity. It was hard to think of it in any other way. She had attended a parent-teacher conference some months earlier and had announced that it was her last; if the school required parental involvement, she said, it wouldn't kill Michaela's father to take a couple hours off work. She was no longer cleaning the house. The rooms gathered dust until Christopher quietly hired a once-a-month cleaning lady. Sometime after this, she stopped cooking. Her expensive set of copper pans collected dust in the kitchen, and her library of cookbooks went unopened. She brought in Chinese takeout or deli sandwiches and started buying disposable plates. The family ate off Styrofoam with plastic forks. There were strange combinations: an enormous container of deli coleslaw with takeout sushi and a container of pickles. Pizza with fortune cookies. Small cartons of milk in lieu of glasses.

Once the dinner was laid out on the table, each one less dinnerlike than the one before, once Michaela and her father were seated, her mother glanced expectantly from one to the other until they started eating. Then she brought out the newspaper and proceeded to ignore both of them.

"*Elaine*," Christopher said.

"I'm sorry, am I being rude?" She put the paper down. "How was work, darling?" She was like an actress impersonating a wife. Something shone terribly in her eyes in those days; she had the look of a woman with a permanent fever. It seemed that she almost never went to sleep.

"Very productive," Christopher said. He no longer recognized this as the life they'd left the circus for, and he felt that there'd been a bait and switch.

"Good." Elaine picked up the paper again.

In the silence after that moment Michaela tried to eat as quickly as possible, or as little as possible, or both. She wanted to leave the table as fast as she could. Her mother put the paper down.

"But no one asked me about my day!" she said. "Don't you want to know what I did?"

"Please," said Michaela's father, "not in front of the kid." He didn't look at Michaela, although she stared at his face.

"Well," she said, "never mind, then. It doesn't matter what I did."

(Notes on the fragility of family, written in his other notebook much later that night: *Everything matters. Everything*

matters. *Do not ever pretend that it doesn't matter what you did.*)
But instead of saying that he just said her name. She snapped
at him and the conversation was carried into the kitchen,
where it billowed up quickly and raged into a storm. This
was the point in the evening when Michaela always left the
table. She went upstairs to her bedroom and did homework
or drew sketches involving tightropes and great expanses of
air. She was plotting the distance to the nearest tree from
her bedroom window, although this was during a period in
her life when she still knew better than to try that kind of
thing. No one at the circus school was allowed to walk on a
tightrope without a safety net or a spotter at the very least,
depending on the height of the rope, and there was a time
in her life when she still understood why this was. The battle
in the kitchen was loud but abstract. It was impossible to
make out the content of what either of her parents was
saying, only the tenor of shrieked accusations and counter-
attacks. There was an evening when she wandered into her
parents' bedroom, perhaps in search of silence, or of clues.
Her mother's clothes were scattered here and there. Her
father's leather bag was lying at the foot of the bed. In the
months since she'd sprained her ankle at the circus school
she had gone through all of her father's files that she could
find, trying to understand what it was that held his attention.

Her father's bag held very little of interest: a wallet, a
comb, an autobiography of an LAPD hostage negotiator,
a beat-up Montreal subway map, a road atlas for the
Southwestern United States, half a pack of du Maurier
cigarettes. But what was strange to her was that it contained
two Bibles, each with a bookmark protruding from the centre
pages. To the best of her recollection she had never attended
a church service, and she had always been under the
impression that her parents were atheists. She opened the
first Bible to the bookmark, and it took a moment to make

out the scrawled message in the dim glow cast by the streetlight outside the window. *Stop looking for me. I'm not missing; I do not want to be found. I wish to remain vanishing. I don't want to go home.—Lilia.*

Her breath caught in her throat. *No,* the missing girl's mother said in a grainy 1987 videotape of a long-archived television episode, *I wish I could forget her.* The pitch of the argument downstairs was changing, moving closer to the foot of the stairs. She tore the page from the Bible, folded it quickly, put it in her pocket and left the room.

20

In the times when Lilia wasn't hiding in the backseat of the car, when there was no one else on the road and the breeze through the passenger-side window was perfect, when she could forget that she was being chased and that she might be found someday, when it was only her father and the radio and the highway—in these times Lilia and her father could talk for hours, and life seemed gorgeous and magnificent and safe. Safety is a car driving quickly away.

He wasn't content with showing her the country. He wanted to show her what he saw in it, to share his private love affair with the sheer beauty of all the details that he could never stop noticing no matter how long he travelled or how fast. When he talked about details—flowers, fences, individual buildings, the poetry hidden in the names of towns—Lilia felt her heart swelling up with an awkward adoration for it all. But she never felt at ease in the world. She couldn't help but think that she wasn't really a part of it, and from the specific night when her memories began (ice against window, lost bunny, snow), the traditions of the world were foreign to her. She picked up what she could from books and television shows, noting carefully the existence of two-parent families, houses, schools, family dogs, memorizing intriguingly home-specific phrases like *latchkey kid* and *back garden* and *state-of-the-art kitchen appliance* and *basement*. She moved over the surface of life the way figure skaters move, fast and choreographed, but she never broke through the ice, she never pierced the surface and descended into those awful beautiful waters, she was never submerged and she never learned to swim in those currents, these currents: all the shadows and light and splendorous horrors that make up the riptides of life on earth.

At the gas stations her father bought magazines. The *New Yorker, Newsweek, Science Times*. These she studied carefully, anthropologically, for information on the world she travelled through. Or he'd buy a book written in a language that she was supposed to be learning at the time (Spanish, Italian, German) and give her an assignment: *By the time we reach St. Louis, kiddo, I'd like a written translation of the first half page.* And she'd bend feverishly over the relevant split-language dictionary (English-German, Español-Inglés, Italiana-Inglese), and he'd give warnings—*Ten miles, kiddo, eight, six, time.* And at the motel that night he'd go over the page with a red pencil while she stared coolly at the television and pretended not to care.

When she was younger she used to tell herself, with some smugness, that some people vanish forever and never are found. Until the interview on *Unsolved Cases*, she still believed herself to be one of them. It wasn't that she ceased to be happy after she saw herself on television, it was that after she saw herself on television she was aware that someday all of this would end.

21

"Dad," Michaela said once, standing at the foot of the stairs while he worked at the dining room table, "can I run away and join the circus?"

Christopher looked up, blinking. He had hardly been home since the page had been torn from the oldest Bible. He couldn't look at his wife without thinking about it, without wondering how she could sabotage him so completely, and so had taken to avoiding her altogether. Michaela looked different somehow, and he realized that she'd gotten a haircut since the last time he'd really looked at her.

"What time is it?" he asked.

"One A.M."

"Don't you have school tomorrow?"

"Yes," she said. "Can I join the circus?"

"You can't join the circus," he replied, annoyed by the question but still grateful to be forced into conversation with her, remembering when he looked at her face that her latest school picture was still in a desk drawer at work. "We've discussed this, remember? A few weeks ago, when you sprained your ankle? The answer's no."

"That was six months ago."

"Six months," he said, and shook his head.

She was staring at him.

"I'm sorry," he said, "the answer's still no."

"But why not?"

"You *know* why not. We already *left* the circus."

When he said it aloud, he felt curiously bereft; he didn't come home very often at all after that, even at night. When her parents didn't come home Michaela sat in the living room, watching television late into the night. One evening a commercial she didn't like came on, and she threw a coffee mug at the screen. The screen cracked with a satisfying pop of light and went dark, and the mug rolled broken under the sofa. After that when she turned on the television the screen lit up but was blue and blank and had a jagged crackling dark line down the centre. Days began to go by when she saw neither of them. She came and went in a house filled with large spaces and shadows, did her laundry sometimes in the evenings in the quiet basement, did her homework in her room at night. She pushed a shopping cart through the wide bright aisles of a grocery store a few blocks away, filling it up with microwave dinners and toaster waffles in a dozen flavours, and spent a great deal of time arranging these in the freezer. She wouldn't have said that she was terribly unhappy. She valued her privacy, and the house was more peaceful without them. She rarely saw her father except in passing; coming out of the upstairs bedroom with a shirt over his arm, going through a box of his files in the dining room. Her mother was prone to coming home at unexpected times—the middle of the afternoon, three A.M., eight in the morning. She had very little to say, right up until the evening when Michaela came home and found her father sitting alone in the dining room with a half-eaten layer cake. The icing was pink.

"You missed the party," her father said. He was leaning as far back as his chair would go without falling over, looking at his hands clasped on the table. He didn't look up at her.

"My birthday isn't for another week," Michaela said. "I'm still fourteen."

"It was a going-away party. Your mother left."

"Left where? Where did she go?"

"I don't know," Christopher said. "She didn't tell me. She just brought home a cake and said she was leaving."

"Did she say when she'd be back?"

"Well, that's just it, pumpkin," he said. "She was a little noncommittal on the subject of whether she was coming back again."

"Did she say why?"

"Apparently I work too much."

Michaela went up to her room then, and closed the door. She didn't go to school the next day, or the day after that. It was much easier to drop out of school than she would have expected, but after a week her father got a phone call from the principal's office and made her go back. A few days later he left a note on her bedside table (*Gone to U.S. on business, back in a couple weeks, keep going to school, will wire grocery money to your chequing account, call Peter if you need anything*) and disappeared. She was used to his business trips, which generally lasted three or four weeks. This time, however, she didn't see him again for a year. When she told Eli this, some years later, he understood that she thought of the quiet dissolution of her family as having been more or less Lilia's fault. Lilia had, after all, written her name in a Bible, and she did run out barefoot into the snow.

"You can see why I hate her," Michaela said.

PART THREE

22

In a hotel room four or five storeys above Boulevard René Lévesque, in the harbour city of Montreal, Eli was trying to find a phone number. Michaela wasn't answering her phone, and he wanted to reach Club Electrolite. He had called directory assistance three or four times, and although the operators themselves seemed flawlessly bilingual, some glitch in the system was causing the phone number to be given repeatedly in French, which was not a language he understood; all the languages he knew were dead or on life support. "Please hold for the number," a sequence of operators had told him brightly, followed by a mechanical click, and then the same robotic *cinq, une, quatre, trois, cinq, deux,* et cetera. "Listen," he was saying to the third or fourth operator, "I need this number in Eng—" but the French robot was already speaking, and he slammed down the receiver in disgust. His collection of obscure aboriginal languages had never seemed more useless. He was reluctant to call the hotel switchboard, because he thought the number he was looking for might belong to a strip club. He stood by the window, disconsolate in the winter sunlight, looking down at the frozen street. He had arrived from New York City by train the night before. He held no Canadian currency. He didn't speak the language.

He had arrived without luggage, the postcard and the envelope folded together in his jacket pocket with his toothbrush and his map. After thirteen hours of travel the train had pulled into a shadowy underworld of tracks and cement platforms, three hours behind schedule, and stopped with a monumental hissing of brakes. He stood for a few minutes on the dim platform, at a loss. He'd had a prolonged disagreement with an imperfectly preserved Amtrak Café Car sandwich earlier in the day, and he still felt a little ill. Travellers moved past him, speaking French. Eli thought about just staying down here, on the level of trains and shadows, boarding the next train bound for New York City and arriving back in Brooklyn sometime tomorrow and just forgetting the whole thing, but decided he'd never forgive himself.

He took a deep breath and started in the direction of the escalators. Across the concrete twilight of the platform, the stairwells held a greenish, somewhat aquatic light. He stepped onto an escalator and travelled upward under exposed fluorescent lights into the cavernous grey of Station Bonaventure. He stood near the top of the escalator for a few minutes, not quite nauseated anymore, but—and this was almost equally uncomfortable—acutely aware of his lack of luggage. He put his hands in his pockets, in the absence of a luggage handle to hold on to, and this was when he realized that he'd left his cell phone on his desk in New York. He swore under his breath and began walking toward the nearest pay-phone sign.

This station was imposing, although he didn't find it beautiful. Blue-and-white frescoes high up on the walls depicted heroic scenes involving swords and canoes. The words of an anthem he'd never heard were rendered in two languages, large enough to be read from below, but there was no other English. The insanity of the journey came over him like a chill. He wanted to go home. He was already wishing he hadn't followed her here. At the pay phone he pulled the envelope from Michaela out of his pocket and dialed the number written on the inside of the flap. It was apparently a cell phone number: there was a shaky, staticky quality to the rings. It rang four or five times before an indifferent-sounding message clicked on: "This is Michaela. Leave a message."

He cleared his throat before the tone. "Michaela," he said, speaking too loudly, "this is Eli Jacobs. I'm in Montreal. I'm coming to the club tomorrow. I'll . . . I'll do what you said, with the white flag and everything, I just . . . I . . . I hope she's there. I hope she's there." He meant to sound stern but sounded nervous. He hung up fast, flustered, and stood for a moment in the phone booth with his eyes closed. Nothing he had known in Brooklyn seemed applicable here.

He forced himself to leave the station, walking out into the cold evening air. The street outside was all but deserted, urban in a way that reminded him of medium-sized cities everywhere. Windswept plazas, hard angles of glass and concrete. Across the street, a low anonymous glass tower reflected lights and the sky. A few cars passed, boxy and random, and it took him a few minutes to recognize them as taxicabs. They weren't yellow. There was, in fact, nothing uniform about them at all; this was a remnant fleet, of every make and colour, all with some variation on a taxi sign bolted to the roof. One or two slowed in front of him. He didn't get in. He thought about calling Geneviève for advice and decided against it.

A couple was approaching through the pools of amber streetlight, passing in and out of shadow and light. The man was telling a complicated story with elaborate hand gestures. The girl let out a high-pitched silvery laugh.

"Excusez-moi," said Eli awkwardly as they drew near. They paused, receptive and looking at him, smiling. His high school French would go no further. "I'm looking for a hotel," he said, conceding linguistic surrender. "Somewhere near here? Could you recommend anything?"

But he'd failed the password test: the air between them turned suddenly to ice. The girl's smile hardened into a sneer. The man said something, but the only words Eli understood were *anglais* and *américain*. Whatever he said made the girl laugh again, but in a different, harder way, and they left him standing and walked onward. The man was resuming his story as they passed out of hearing range. The girl was laughing her original silvery laugh. *"Wouldn't you like to see what it really means to live in a city with a doomed language?"* Geneviève had asked him once, some days or weeks ago in what may have been another lifetime. He stared down at the glittering sidewalk, blinking and at a loss, while the barely recognizable taxicabs kept passing like clockwork in front of him, a looped reel with minor variations (Ford, Toyota, Toyota, Chevrolet), and it occurred to him that Thomas was right, that coming here had been a colossal mistake and also that he was somehow already too far in.

When he turned back toward the train station, he saw that there was a hotel attached to it. The Queen Elizabeth Hotel towered just behind him. The lobby coincided with some uninformed ideas he had about what grand hotels might have looked like in Russia, circa 1960 or so: red carpets, gold-and-crystal chandeliers, a handful of businessmen in double-breasted suits, older women with sculpted hair and small handbags waiting stoically on ornate sofas here and there among the pillars. The room was warm with cigar smoke and conversation. He couldn't understand a single word. It turned out that rooms were startlingly inexpensive in the wintertime.

In the morning he spent a long time in the shower. When he got out he dug in his jacket pocket for the folded envelope and dialed Michaela's number again. It went immediately to voice mail. He hung up without speaking and went down to the front desk to ask for directions. The lobby was much less pleasant in daylight. The concierge tactfully steered him away from Club Electrolite but recommended a number of fine restaurants and a jazz club nearby. A bellboy, apparently concluding that he was yet another American tourist here for the sex, pulled him aside and said he thought Club Electrolite was near the corner of Sainte-Catherine and Rue McGill but remarked that as far as he knew it was primarily a dance club with some go-go dancers, and that if Eli wanted to see some, ahem, *danseuses nues* perhaps (irritating wink here), he needn't walk that far; he could, the bellboy said helpfully, simply make his way to Rue Sainte-Catherine, where apparently there were two or three strip clubs on any given block from here to the city limits. In both directions.

"No, I'm looking for a girl," Eli said.

"Of course," said the bellboy.

"No, a specific girl. I'm looking for a specific girl."

"Aren't we all?" said the bellboy. "Listen, go to Club Electrolite if you want, but you go a couple blocks east on St. Catherine Street around nightfall, you'll see all the girls money can buy. But don't go too far east or they all turn into transvestites by the time you get to Rue de la Visitation."

Eli thanked him and set out for the address on the postcard. It was just past noon, but the sky was heavy and dark. Snow was beginning to fall, and the sidewalk was slippery. He walked slowly, not particularly eager to arrive at his destination, and he'd walked a half block past the club before he realized his mistake and doubled back to find it.

Club Electrolite was a narrow four-storey building of the same dirty grey stone as the buildings around it. The door was locked. A neon sign flashed the outline of a naked angel above the door, but all the windows were dark. Eli pulled at the door again before he noticed the sign on the door. The sign, miraculously bilingual, advised him that the club had switched recently to winter hours and would be open only on Thursday, Friday, and Saturday nights until May.

That was the third Monday afternoon in December. Eli wandered until he found a warm café, and sat alone for some time with a coffee and the remains of his thoughts.

IN THE LAST LIGHT of afternoon, a few days later, Eli took a walk to the river. Thirteen hours by train to the south, New York City was etched in the brilliance of late autumn, but here winter was well under way. It had snowed twice already in the days since he'd arrived, and the temperature seemed to be dropping by the hour. A white electric cross burned at night high up on the hill above the city. Eli, looking out from the window of the Queen Elizabeth Hotel, thought it was one of the loneliest visions he'd ever seen. He walked for entire afternoons through the frozen streets looking for Lilia, standing in places that he thought might attract her, sitting in coffee shops where he thought she might linger, reading the English-language press for clues on the city he found himself in, trying not to speak English in public except when ordering coffee. The businesses closed early here, but he found two coffee shops about a mile apart that stayed open all night, admitting freezing drafts every time the door opened. He thought of them as beacons in the night ocean and moved between them on alternate nights. Cold air seeped through the windows of every room.

He had read somewhere that there was a cruise ship docked at the port. He wasn't particularly interested in seeing it, but it seemed like something Lilia might take pictures of, and on the fourth day he thought that walking there and then walking back to the hotel might take up a few hours, and he was desperate to distract himself. Club Electrolite was theoretically opening again that night, and he hadn't decided what he was going to say when he saw her. He was walking slowly through the oldest part of the city, moving south toward the harbour, when a movement high above him in an alleyway caught his eye: a girl was standing on the railing of a fire escape. She was balanced perfectly two storeys above the cobblestones, one hand steadying her on the ladder above. For a confused moment he took her for a suicide, but at the instant he was about to call out to her, he saw the rope. It had been strung tight from building to building, tied expertly across the vertiginous span between fire escapes. He would have taken it for a makeshift clothesline, except for the girl. He saw the way she had aligned her thin body with the rope, the ballet slippers on her feet and the ferocity of her obvious intent, and he understood what she was going to do. He drifted a few steps into the alleyway and sank close against a brick wall, looking up.

He wanted to call out, perhaps to stop her, but it occurred to him that it was too late, that any sudden noise or movement might be fatally distracting. The timing of his arrival on the scene was impeccable. As he stood below, cold sweat on his forehead, she casually removed her hand from the ladder. Eli glanced back at the street; a man passed on the other side, looking at his reflection in a long blank office-building window, and Eli thought to call out to him with the best high school French he knew—*Help me, aidez-moi, s il vous plaît, please*—but what could another man do at this moment besides distract her into a lethal fall? She was well beyond anyone's reach.

She took one careful, expert step out onto the tightrope. He closed his eyes to avoid seeing the inevitable: the loss of balance, unbearable teetering, nightmare wingless descent. Surely no one survived this. A rope with no safety net and cobblestones beneath; he could already see the conspiracy unfolding between the rope and the cobblestones and the siren call of gravity, blood pooling outward from the shattered skull. His hands were clenched fists in his pockets. He wanted to leave and spare himself the vision. *But no one*, Zed had scrawled once in a letter from Africa several years ago, *should have to die without a witness*. Eli forced himself to look at her.

She took a second impeccable slow-motion step, and then another. Her face was unreadable and utterly calm. For the first time he began to notice what she looked like, beyond the obvious horror of watching her last moments on earth. It was hard to see her clearly from this angle, in this light, but she was wearing a red dress, and her hair was platinum-white: she shone like a signal in the high shadows above. An apparition, and the poetry of her balance: she moved so slowly. This was a terrible, nerve-shattering meditation she practised. He couldn't breathe. One deliberate step after another and she was halfway across already, two-thirds of the way, unceasing, and then she reached out and grasped the fire-escape ladder across the alley from where she'd started, safe and balanced on the opposite railing. She hopped down to the fire-escape landing and then stood there looking down, almost directly above him. Safe.

There were tears on his face. His hand was trembling when he brushed them away, and his heart was beating too fast. He was furious. She climbed down the fire stairs in one continuous movement and dropped down lightly onto the top of a Dumpster. From there it was an easy leap to the cobble-stones, where she'd left a shiny silver jacket and a pair of high-heeled boots in a bundle by the wall. She took off the ballet slippers and put them in a jacket pocket. It seemed that the zipper on her left boot was broken, but she had a shoestring that she tied around her ankle to keep it up. She looked up at Eli then, and held his gaze while she pulled on the jacket. Strange creature: beautiful, he supposed. She had short hair that stood on end, a struck-by-lightning look, shocked colourless. This close, he saw that her eyes were green. There was a sweet, slightly decrepit smell about her, like hair gel and stale perfume and cigarettes.

"You were looking up my skirt," she said flatly, in accentless English. She was slightly out of breath.

There was a look in her eyes that struck him as unhealthy. Eli swallowed hard, with enormous effort, and shook his head.

"I wasn't looking up your skirt. I was just standing here, and I saw you." He felt dazed and sick, and his voice sounded strange to him.

"Right," she said. "You were just standing there, looking up my skirt."

Eli was in no mood to argue. He'd just seen her die, whether she was still breathing or not. He looked up at the tightrope, ingeniously knotted and suddenly innocuous; if he'd chanced upon it now, he'd assume it was a clothesline. For a moment it wasn't at all clear to him that it *wasn't* a clothesline, that he wasn't dreaming and wouldn't wake up in a moment in his bed in Brooklyn with Lilia asleep beside him. He took a slow step backward, closed his eyes for a moment, and touched the fingertips of both hands fleetingly to his forehead. His shoulder came up hard against a brick wall.

"Did you cut your hair recently?" she asked.

"I'm sorry," Eli said hoarsely. "I just don't feel like talking to you anymore. I'm not feeling that well. If you'll excuse me . . ."

"No, wait," she said, "did you cut your hair recently? Was it longer before?"

He stopped backing away and looked at her. She was considering him, frowning, like someone trying to recall a forgotten name.

"Yes," he said. "It was longer before."

"I've seen you," she said. "I've seen you before somewhere."

"I very much doubt that."

"No, I've seen you before somewhere." She smiled suddenly. "Oh God, oh God, it's *you*," she said. "Of all people. Did you know Lilia once took a picture of you while you were sleeping?"

He couldn't speak.

"But in the picture," she said, "you did have slightly longer hair. You're the absolute last person I expected to run into here. Although I did think I might see you tonight." She was moving past him, still smiling. "The club opens at nine," she said. "I will see you there, won't I? Lilia said she'd be there tonight."

"Michaela," he said. "Michaela, wait—"

But she blew him a kiss from just outside the alleyway, and when he walked out after her he couldn't tell which way she'd gone, in all the narrow ancient streets.

Christopher left the city quietly, at an hour of the day when Michaela should have been home from school but wasn't. She was smoking cigarettes behind the school gym as his car pulled out of the driveway and had only just arrived home as he approached the American border. She was tearing his note into furious pieces as he was entering the United States. He'd told Peter that he was leaving town for a few weeks and asked him to look in on Michaela occasionally. He convinced himself that the arrangement wasn't unreasonable. It was true that Michaela was only fifteen, he thought, but his daughter was never in any trouble that he heard about and didn't seem to need him anyway.

He was waved across the border and drove quickly into the United States, feeling lighter than he had in years. He was deep into Upstate New York by evening. He spent that night in a beige-and-pink Ramada Hotel room that still smelled of new carpeting. He couldn't sleep. At three in the morning he got up and spent some time looking at a map. The town of Leonard, Arizona, was circled in green. He went to bed at four and woke two hours later from a dream of ringing pay phones, strangely rested. He was travelling again an hour later, driving quickly south.

Lilia was aware at times of a presence half glimpsed alongside her, evanescent, only indirectly apparent, like the stars you can see only when you look away. A blue car passed them on the highway, the driver staring indifferently at the road ahead, and she was unable to escape the impression that she'd seen him before somewhere. Or as she emerged blinking from a restaurant into the blinding noon sunlight, a man stepped into a hardware store across the street. Did he have the same profile as the driver who had passed them? The sound of a door closing quietly on an upstairs motel balcony, just at the moment she emerged from the room. Footsteps on the same balcony at four A.M. An inescapable feeling, as she pulled the cord on the pale motel curtains, of having just severed someone's line of sight. A waitress seated Lilia and her father at a restaurant table, and she realized that an uneaten meal had been abandoned at the table beside them, along with a twenty-dollar bill. The puzzled waitress returned a few minutes later and took the plate away, pocketed the twenty, and it wouldn't have been that remarkable except that Lilia had seen the same thing on a table in another town two days ago, and she couldn't help but imagine that the same person had abandoned both meals just at the instant she'd walked into the restaurant.

In short, she dwelt for some time in the hinterland between sheer paranoia and reasonable suspicion, but she didn't mention it to her father. It was only since the town of Leonard that she'd sensed this shadow travelling alongside her, and while it was possible that she was imagining it, it was equally possible that she had conjured her pursuer out of the ether with a phone call. She remembered the cool plastic of the receiver against her face, the crackle of static down the wires, the clicking sounds as the Arizona pay phone forged a fragile link with a telephone somewhere in southern Quebec, and she wondered if her mother's phone was tapped. It didn't seem unreasonable. Lilia watched enough television to think it more than plausible that calls to a kidnapped child's home of origin might be recorded, or followed up on and traced at the very least. On an ocean of static, she had sent up a flare.

Lilia spent some time wondering whether her father had noticed the new pursuer. It occurred to her after a while that even if he suspected the same things she did, he might not notice the difference—he had always been aware of shadows, although it had never been clear whether they were real or not. He had always hidden his child in the backseats of moving automobiles. He had always glanced over his shoulder and beaten nervous waltz rhythms on the steering wheel with his hands, driven through the night and taken looped circuitous routes to throw off potential pursuers, thought up names and alibis and procured forged driver's licences and birth certificates when necessary, managed the web of interlinked bank accounts that kept their tenuous existence afloat. He had always been followed by shadows and ghosts. Whether or not they were real was almost incidental. The waters were always rising behind them, and he was always carrying her to higher ground. The realization made Lilia's heart swell awkwardly with love and guilt, and she couldn't bring herself to mention this latest shade. He didn't mention it either, but then, he also didn't stop. By unspoken agreement, they no longer stayed anywhere longer than two or three nights. There were motel rooms, diners, endless chain restaurants, pasta cooked in hotel kitchenettes, hours of highway passing under the wheels. They lingered in public only rarely. An hour in a park, instead of an entire afternoon. An hour in a library, instead of a day. When she emerged from gas station restrooms, he was waiting outside the door. He didn't let her stay alone in the car in parking lots anymore. Lilia walked beside him into every gas station, every store. He was always beside her. She was seldom alone. She noticed lines on his face that hadn't been there before. And sometimes she had the impression, walking back through the parking lot to the car with an armload of groceries and magazines, of being watched through one of the other windshields.

25

It was a long time before Eli could bring himself to leave the hotel that night. He spent the evening lying in bed at the hotel with a Do Not Disturb sign on the outside door handle, staring up at the ceiling. At eight o'clock he ordered a room-service dinner. He ate a dinner roll and a forkful of chicken, suddenly couldn't stand the idea of eating, put the tray outside in the hallway, and ordered a cup of coffee. This he drank standing at the window, looking down at the grey roofscape and the deserted street below. The idea of seeing Lilia again was disconcerting. He had been dwelling increasingly on the way she'd walked out. Since she'd left without her suitcase but it had been gone from under the bed, she had to have planted it somewhere the night before—the janitor's closet by the front door? The basement of the building? A locker at the train station? The premeditation was awful. Horrific to think of her sleeping beside him that last night, already packed for departure and planning on disappearing in the morning. He stood for a long time in the shower, perfectly still in the stream of scalding water. He put on a new shirt that he'd bought earlier in the day and stood for a while staring motionless at his face in the mirror. "This is what I came here for," he told his reflection, but his reflection didn't look convinced. He set out for Club Electrolite at ten o'clock, but when he stepped outside the day's trampled snow had frozen on the sidewalk into a sheet of uneven dark ice. It was midnight before he came to the door.

The main dance floor of Club Electrolite was vast and shadowy, with a few small round stages for go-go dancers scattered at regular intervals across it. The mirrored walls gave a queasy impression of infinity. Spinning lights illuminated pale clouds of dry ice that hissed from the corners of the room, and a scattering of disco balls threw shards of light back from the ceiling. The darkness was old here; it had always been night. He checked his coat and made his way slowly through the crowd, past the bar, onto the dance floor. He didn't feel like drinking. He made no effort to dance. He stood near a speaker, hands in his pockets, and the music was so loud that he thought he might die. His clothing moved in the gale of sound. He wanted to lie down and let the sound wash over him. He wanted to surrender. He tried to look at every face in the crowd, but Lilia was nowhere.

There was a boy standing near him with a trumpet, playing barely audible counterpoint to the techno beat. He was thin and strung out, wild-eyed in the lights. His hair stood on end. Whoever was in charge of the lighting clearly liked him; a spotlight caught his trumpet in a long gleam of light. Eli stood watching him, hands in his pockets, wondering what to do. There was only one go-go dancer tonight. Michaela was clad in black vinyl, gyrating on a stage near the centre of the room. She writhed and shimmered, intoxicated by herself. He realized that she couldn't see him in the crowd and realized at the same moment that he'd forgotten the white flag. For a moment something was breaking inside him, and he pressed both hands to his forehead and closed his eyes, but all wasn't lost after all—an idea caught him and he moved toward the blue-lit bar on the far wall. The bartender had left a white towel on the bar. Eli ordered a drink, and then the moment her back was turned he slid the towel quickly from the counter and slipped back into the crowd. He made his way to a place not far from Michaela, trying to look at every face at once in case Lilia might be here, and raised the white towel with both hands over his head. A spotlight, moving over the crowd, caught the towel and transformed it into a rectangle of ultraviolet light. He looked up at it, awkwardly conspicuous, and then back at the dancer. Michaela was watching him, expressionless, still dancing. She raised one thin arm over her head and snapped her fingers in the air.

The music lowered slightly, and the MC's smooth voice broke over the melody. The room was flooded suddenly in black light. Every white T-shirt in the room and Eli's improvised flag turned violently luminescent.

"*Bon soir, madames et monsieurs.* Good evening, ladies and gentlemen, *et bienvenue à Club Electrolite.* We have a special message this evening . . . our lovely dancer *ce soir, notre Michaela*, would like to welcome Eli Jacobs to the club."

Eli lowered the bar towel and stood stunned and helpless while the swirling of lights resumed and the crowd (mostly drunk, only half aware that there'd been a brief interruption) again began moving to the rising beat. The spotlight trained on him, however, didn't move. Eli didn't move either. He stood frozen and illuminated, singled out. Someone tapped his shoulder. He turned, and the bartender snatched her towel from his hand and shouted something at him in French. It was hard to see her clearly through the haze of light as she walked away from him. When he looked back Michaela had vanished. The pedestal stage stood abandoned and suddenly unlit. An arm emerged from the crowd and set an empty beer bottle on its surface. The boy with the trumpet resumed his inaudible melody.

Eli stood still, and the music rose around him. Michaela appeared at his side and took his hand. He followed her like a child as she forced her way through the crowd, speaking over her shoulder. The music was too loud and he couldn't hear what she was saying; still, he followed her through the half-hidden door beside the DJ booth. Her hand was damp with sweat. On the other side of the door a bouncer sat reading on the staircase landing, leaning back in a rickety-looking wooden chair under an exposed light bulb that shivered with every beat. He glanced up disinterestedly from *Tropique du Cancer* and nodded them down the stairs. The music grew quieter as they descended, until at the foot of the stairs it had become pure vibration, sensed rather than heard, like a complicated heartbeat coming from above. The Club Electrolite basement was a cramped, labyrinthine space, all cheap wooden doors and plywood walls. Wires brushed against him from the ceiling. He trailed after her, she called Lilia's name, she flung open one of the doors and pulled him into an empty dressing room.

"Well?" Eli said.

Michaela dropped his hand, drew a deep breath, and swore softly. She sat down at a makeup counter, stared at herself in the mirror for a second, and then a sweep of her arm sent the makeup to the floor in a storm of silver tubes and tiny jars that broke open and spilled out bright powders and iridescent goo. Altogether, it was a beautiful mess. He stood leaning against the door frame watching her while she covered her face with both hands and sat very still for a moment.

"I'm sorry," she said finally. She blinked a few times, caught sight of her red-eyed reflection in the mirror and winced, cast around in the mess on the floor for a tissue. When she found one she dabbed at the mascara streaks on her face, gazing steadily into her own eyes in the mirror. "It's just that I expected her to be here."

He cleared his throat, but she didn't look at him.

"Where is she?"

"She was here a half hour ago. We had a fight, but I told her not to leave."

"Why did you bring me here? Are you a friend of hers?"

She made a brittle sound that could have been a laugh. "I wouldn't say that *friend* is exactly the word, really." Her eyes were glassy and bloodshot in the mirror. "I don't think she likes me very much."

"That page from the Bible," he said, "the Twenty-second Psalm with her handwriting on it. Where did that come from?"

"She wrote that when she was seven or eight," said Michaela, "in a hotel room somewhere in the States. *I wish to remain vanishing.* I always liked that line."

"But why did you have it?"

"Because my father had it. He was the detective on the case."

"I don't understand . . ."

"Well, it's complicated." She was reapplying eyeliner. "He was the detective on the case, and I read all his notes."

"Can you just tell me where Lilia is, and I'll get out of here?"

"She'll come back to me," she said, ignoring the question. "I'm the only one who knows her story. I'm her only witness."

"What are you talking about?"

"Listen," she said, "I have to go back onstage."

"Can you at least tell me why I had to raise up that bloody white dish towel? I felt like an idiot."

"How else was I supposed to see you in the crowd? The black lights pick up everything white. I didn't think I'd run into you in the old city this afternoon." Someone pounded briefly on the door of her dressing room. "I have to go back up," she said. "Can you meet me somewhere later?"

"Anywhere," he said.

She arrived at the coffee shop on Boulevard Saint-Laurent just after two A.M., shivering her way out of a cab and sinking into a chair across the table from him. She said she was exhausted. She closed her eyes, and he took the opportunity to study her up close. She had a small faint scar on her forehead, imperfectly camouflaged with makeup. She was beautiful in a way that suggested very little time for beauty left ahead of her; there was a hardness and an exhaustion already settling over her face. Eli leaned forward across the table, close enough to smell the cigarette smoke in her hair.

"It's two in the morning," he said softly, "I've been here for days, and I don't speak the language. I just want to talk to Lilia and make sure she's all right. I am very tired, and I need you to be straight with me. Can you tell me where she is?"

She opened her eyes. "How long did it take you to get here?"

"Thirteen hours."

"Jesus. Did you walk?"

"I took the train. Could you tell me where she is?"

"I've never been to Brooklyn," she said after some time had passed. She was quiet for a few seconds, staring out the window. "She told you she was abducted?"

"As a child. Yes."

"You know what's amazing? She doesn't know why she was abducted. Only that she was. It's incredible, what the mind can block. She wrote to me from New York City a few weeks ago."

"She wrote you?"

"Maybe a month ago. I told her I wouldn't tell her anything unless she came here."

"You forced her to come here. Do you have any idea—"

"No," Michaela said, "I *suggested* that she come here. Don't raise your voice, or I will walk out of here and you will never see her again. She came here all by herself."

He leaned back in his chair, looking out the window. The city had reached the stage of night when the taxicabs were appearing, ferrying the worn-out glittering nightlife home from the clubs.

"I don't understand why she had to come here," he said finally. "Whatever it is she wanted to know, couldn't you have told her over the phone?"

"I wanted to meet her. I'd known about her half my life. But listen, I brought you here for a reason. I have to ask you something, and I want you to answer me honestly. There's an argument that I was having with her, very recently."

"How recently?"

"A few hours ago, just before I saw you on the dance floor. We were talking about a car accident. Did she ever speak to you about a car accident?"

"What?"

"An *accident*," she repeated patiently, "involving a *car*, that would have occurred when she'd just turned sixteen. Maybe two or three days after her sixteenth birthday. Because it's absolutely imperative that you tell me if she did, if she told you anything about it, if you know anything, anything at all. I have to know." Michaela clasped her hands on the tabletop, and he saw that her knuckles were red from the cold.

"What could a car accident that happened when she was sixteen possibly have to do with you?"

She just looked at him.

"No," Eli said. "She didn't tell me anything about that. I don't know anything about a car accident."

"I don't believe you."

"Well, I suppose that's your choice. Listen, I'm tired, and I want to get out of here. Can you tell me where she is?"

"I read my father's case notes," Michaela said. "My father was, well, let's say my father was a little obsessed. The ironic thing is, I know everything about her life except the one thing that I really want to know. I even know the things she doesn't."

"I'm not following you. How could you know things about her life that she doesn't?"

"I know why she has those scars on her arms, for instance. Do you?"

"No," Eli said. "I never asked."

"Even if you'd asked," she said, "Lilia couldn't have told you."

"She doesn't know?"

"She doesn't remember."

He was silent, watching her.

"I know Lilia's story," she said. "I know why she was abducted, I know what happened to her before her father took her away, I know all the things that she can't remember herself. I offered them to her in exchange for telling me about the accident, but she wouldn't. She wouldn't tell me about it, even though I could tell she wanted to know what had happened to her, and we argued horribly about it earlier. But she told you her story, didn't she?"

"Yes. No. All of her story except that."

"Tell me about the accident," she said, "and I will tell you where she is."

"I don't want to use Lilia's story as a bargaining chip."

"But what else do you have?"

Eli looked at her across the table until she stood up and kissed him on the forehead and told him to meet her here again same time tomorrow and then maybe they could talk, and then she was gone in a blast of cold air through the closing glass doors. And it was hard to say later how any moment this ghastly could possibly become a routine, but he knew no one else in the city, and she knew where Lilia was. He waited for her every night after that in the all-night coffee house on the corner of Boulevard Saint-Laurent and Rue Prince-Arthur, drinking coffee by the window and watching for her shape, for the platform boot emerging from the cab or the narrow figure walking slowly up the hill. She came in exhausted but strangely bright, sometimes feverish, glassy-eyed. She smiled wanly when she saw him, two or three or four A.M., and slid into the opposite chair. She had a curious smell about her at this hour, especially if she'd been in the VIP lounge on the second floor: hairspray, men's cologne, her perfume. Other, subtler notes that he preferred not to identify too closely. Her hair had softened by this time of night, and her makeup was blurred. There was a loose, dangerous quality to her movements. Her face was flushed. It was sometimes a long time before she spoke.

"Are you all right?"

"Of course," Michaela said, but in those moments her smile seemed empty, her eyes unfocused. He wanted to press her for Lilia's location, to somehow force her to produce Lilia from thin air, but it was impossible: there was something broken in her, something exposed and open to the elements that made forcing her to do anything seem almost un-thinkable. She claimed she didn't know where Lilia was. Then she amended this and claimed that she did know where Lilia was but that she wouldn't tell him unless he told her about the car accident. She claimed that Lilia was still in the city but that she wasn't sure where. Then she claimed that Lilia was going to reappear at the moment they least expected, but the moment they least expected never seemed to come, and days passed slowly in the startling cold.

"Can I get you something?"

She wanted tea. A day or two earlier Eli had bought a dictionary and a phrasebook and figured out how to order tea in what he believed to be reasonably passable French, but the barista invariably replied in English no matter which language he tried to use. It seemed clear that this was a rejection of some kind, but he hadn't decided whether it was a rejection of the English language or a rejection of him personally, and either way it was exhausting and he preferred not to think about it. He went to the counter and came back with tea and she sipped at it, looking away from him, her mind elsewhere. She looked out the window and told him again how she'd like to travel away from here, but in the week that he'd known her Eli had heard this monologue four or five times, and he was quickly running out of sympathetic comments. He could only nod and watch her light another cigarette.

"There's something I don't understand," Eli said. "How did Lilia know who you are?"

"What?"

"To write you the letter. You said she wrote to you from New York."

"Oh." She was quiet for a moment. "It isn't entirely accurate to say she wrote to me, actually." She took a long drag of her cigarette. Her eyes were troubled. "It was a letter to my father. I got a call from the private investigative agency, maybe a month and a half ago. They said he'd left six months earlier and they didn't have a forwarding address for him, and they didn't know what to do with all his mail. I was hoping maybe someone had sent him money, so I went there and picked up his mail and opened all of it. It was mostly junk, but there was a letter from Lilia."

"What did she write?"

"She requested a truce. She said she was tired of always being followed and watched."

"She was being followed?"

"All her life," Michaela said.

Lilia turned fourteen in a small city in Illinois, and her father gave her a camera. Her first shot was out the window of the chain restaurant where she was eating birthday cake, at the movie theatre blinking across the wide evening street. Somewhere near Indianapolis she knelt down by the side of the road to take a picture of a sign with the paint peeling off— Farm-Fresh Corn and Tomatoes—and found beauty in the worn wood and faded lettering. She developed the film after that at one-hour photo places, loitering around shopping malls until the pictures were ready, and pored over them in the car, in a park, in the motel room at night. The pictures gave her a sense of continuity, of a record being constructed. Lilia had been in flight for seven years now, travelling quickly, and it was a bright pleasure to have a means of capturing the flight path. She took pictures of signs, mostly, although not signs that could be traced easily to any particular place. She especially liked signs with misspellings, or with the paint peeling off. She liked taking very wide shots of deserted streets, and pictures of cars approaching from great distances away.

Lilia was allowed to take pictures of anything except herself and her father. "We must be careful," he warned, "about the accumulation of evidence."

Michaela was always running out of cigarettes. She coughed dryly sometimes, in a rasping way, and the spasms brightened the red veins of her eyes. Her eyes were almost always red, even when sober, because she couldn't sleep. She would do anything to avoid being alone at night with her insomnia, and Eli was willing to go to great lengths to avoid being alone in general, so they sat together in the café at the corner, watching the gradual progression of night. The night passed through stages: first the crowds of beautiful strangers in the electric midnight, enthusiastic and painted and dressed for the clubs, then the fleet of mismatched taxicabs at the intersection, and later an inky blackness, these last few hours of night, four in the morning and the occasional drunken kid stumbling by with a slice of greasy pizza, a girl with fishnet stockings and vacant eyes weaving over the sidewalk, the cold amber of streetlights on pavement and ice. After the taxis passed, wave upon wave, the streets went quiet till morning. The city slept uneasily, under the sign of the cross: it shone in brilliant white high up on the hillside outside Eli's hotel-room window, a charm over the wide blank streets and deserted sidewalks and shadowy parks.

Michaela laughed softly to herself, said something inaudible. She was dazed and tired in the afternoons, sharp and lucid in the evenings, and slipping into incoherence by three A.M.

"What did you say? I couldn't hear you."

"My parents were in a travelling circus," she told him, gorgeous and exhausted and coming undone sometime between three and four o'clock in the morning. "Did I tell you that?"

"A couple of times, yes. It's kind of unbelievable."

"Isn't it? A family of actual circus people. My grandparents too," she said. "Both sides. Do you believe the desire to travel is genetic?"

"You sound like Lilia."

Her name broke the conversation and they stayed together for a long time in silence. The moon was setting behind the rooftops on the other side of Boulevard Saint-Laurent. They had had the same argument every night for a week: Michaela wasn't going to tell him where Lilia was unless he told her about the accident. Strange limbo. Michaela lit a new cigarette off the end of the old one and then dropped the old one into the last few drops of her tea. She turned the still-warm glass between her hands for a while, smoking, looking down at the extinguished ashes. She smoked with the practiced elegance of a career smoker, one who was perhaps born holding a cigarette and doesn't mind admitting that she smokes rather well.

"She travelled beautifully," she said finally.

"You're the only person I've ever met who actually literally chain smokes," Eli said.

"She's a bit like a ghost," said Michaela, still thinking of Lilia. "What was it like, living with her?"

"She was different from anyone I've ever . . . she had strange habits," he said. "She was unsettling. But sometimes there was something perfect about it."

"All of it?"

"Of course not all of it. Nothing's perfect all the time."

"What, then?"

"The times we were alone. We spent a lot of time alone in the apartment, or out walking, and there was this silence that'd fall between us, and I know this sounds . . . I know this sounds stupid or absurd, but it was perfect. I can't explain it any better than that. The silence was perfect."

"Silence? What else?"

"We had these friends in Brooklyn—actually, *I* had these friends, she didn't have friends, she came out of thin air with a suitcase—anyway, I had these friends who thought they were artists. Well, I don't know, maybe they were. Maybe we were. I can't judge it anymore, what we were doing there. I didn't think that what we were doing was good enough at the time, but maybe it was. I don't know."

She watched him without speaking.

"You know what bothered me about it? Everyone was supposedly committed to the pursuit of truth and beauty, or at least one of those things, but no one was actually doing anything about it, and it seemed all wrong to me. The inertia, I mean. The inertia made everything seem fraudulent. There we were, talking about art, but no one was *doing* anything except Lilia. She was taking pictures. She spoke four languages."

"Five."

"You're counting Russian? Anyway, what I'm saying is that no one was doing anything important except her. She worked as a dishwasher, she lived cheaply, she took beautiful pictures and translated things. She never made any money off it, it was just something she did. The point is, she never talked about it. She never seemed like she was posing. She never theorized or deconstructed. She just practised her art, practised it instead of analyzing it to death, and it rendered the rest of us fraudulent. There aren't many people in the world . . ." He stopped talking and shook his head. He didn't trust himself to continue.

Michaela was silent for a moment, looking down at her hands. "I have a picture she took," she said finally, "if you'd like to see it." She was reaching for her purse at her feet. She put it on the table, the fake leather gleaming under the café lights, pulled an envelope from a secret inside pocket and passed it to him.

The corners of the envelope were softened with wear. It held a single black-and-white photograph of Michaela and Lilia standing side by side before the mirror of a public washroom, a line of cubicle doors open behind them. Lilia held her camera just below her face with both hands. There were dark circles under her eyes, and her face was serious and still. Michaela, beside her, was smiling slightly, and both of them were watching Lilia's eyes in the mirror.

"Where was this taken?" He couldn't stop his voice from shaking. He was looking into Lilia's eyes for a trace of something, remorse perhaps, but of course she could have been thinking of anything.

"Here," she said. "In the washroom at the back." She took the photograph from him, put it back in the envelope, and put the envelope back in the secret pocket in her bag.

28

The year Michaela was fifteen, she lived alone. Her father was travelling in another country.

Christopher was moving quickly. He was having strange dreams about cars and pay phones. He had never felt so clear. In a mountainous state in the middle of the country, he realized that he'd fallen into Lilia's wake. He'd felt himself for a long time to be moving closer to her, drawing near as he circled outward from the town of Leonard, Arizona, but it still seemed faintly miraculous when the trail suddenly became clear. At first he didn't believe it. But a woman at a quiet rural gas station said that yes, upon reflection, she did seem to recall a man and his daughter passing through yesterday morning with suitcases in the back of the car, and a clerk at a motel down the highway said the same thing. He trailed them down into Florida, through Miami, then up into a semi-urban hinterland of highway overpasses and towns with wide empty streets, straggly palm trees, blank almost identical houses set far back from the street. He followed them silently, travelling alongside, propelled and haunted by visions and dreams. He moved alone and weightless over several Midwestern states, just behind or sometimes alongside the fugitives, just out of sight. He had always had an intuition stronger than any of his senses, and it seemed that it had hardened and crystallized into something formidable. What he found, and this was both disturbing and miraculous (that word again, but no other word came to him when he thought of it), was that after he'd seen them for the first time (emerging like apparitions from a chain restaurant in a small city in Illinois on Lilia's birthday, climbing back into their car, Lilia stopping first to take a photograph of the street) he always knew where they were.

Sometimes he gave them a head start, to test himself: an hour, a day. He'd stay in his motel room, reading in solitude for long periods; he bought books in the towns he passed through, histories and biographies mostly, and left them behind in motel rooms when he was done with them. The only books he kept were battered copies of *Bullfinch's Mythology* and *The Complete Plays of Shakespeare*, and the two Bibles in which Lilia had written. One of these was missing the original note, of course, but he had a photocopy folded into the back page. It was the Shakespeare that he went back to most frequently; he had been reading *Twelfth Night* back when he'd first taken Lilia's case, and there was something soothing about the continuity. He would read for a while and later he would check out of the motel room and drive after them, and find as he travelled that he knew where they'd gone. Sure enough, he'd see their latest car in a motel parking lot, or drive past on the street of the next town as they walked together. He felt that he could exist this way forever. Just behind them, watching over them, travelling alongside, aware of their every move, able to bring them in at any time. He didn't have to do anything. The connection was effortless. His family was suspended. It was as though they'd disappeared. Weeks passed when he didn't think of them. It was a beautiful state of limbo to be in.

Six months after Christopher had left his daughter in Montreal he pulled over to the side of the road in Oklahoma after a full day of driving, a little lost, and stared hard at the horizon for a while to clear his head. That was the first time he realized how long he'd been gone. In the next town he wired money to his daughter's chequing account and kept driving.

29

On Eli's third week in the city he thought he heard Lilia's name. It was one A.M. at the Café Depot, and he was waiting alone for Michaela to arrive. He looked up at the two girls speaking French at a nearby table, but waited until one stood up to leave before he made his approach.

"*Excusez-moi*," he said awkwardly, to the girl remaining.

She looked up and smiled. "You sound like you'd prefer to speak English," she said.

He found himself smiling back. "I would," he admitted. "Thank you."

"I've seen you here a few times," she said.

"I'm sorry to disturb you. It's just that I've been looking for someone in the city, a friend, and I thought I heard you say her name just now. Lilia?"

She shook her head, still smiling but puzzled, and then brightened suddenly. "*Lillian*," she said. "Lillian Bouchard. We were just talking about her. That was the name you heard."

"Oh," he said. "I'm sorry, I didn't mean to . . ."

"It's all right," she said. She extended a hand. "Ondine. Where are you from?"

"Eli." Her hand was soft and warm in his own. "Visiting from New York."

"New York," she said vaguely, and he understood from her smile that she'd never been. "First time in Montreal?"

He nodded.

"Welcome to the city," she said.

"Thank you," he said. "I'd ask you to join me, but I'm meeting someone . . ."

"It's all right," she said. "I'll see you again sometime. I hope you find her."

"Thank you."

He returned to his table and sat with his back to her, looking out at the cold grey street. He waited for Michaela every night until three A.M., until four, knowing she would eventually appear. Or he sometimes stood against a wall at Club Electrolite, watching her movements on her tiny stage, looking for Lilia in the crowd. The crowd barely noticed Michaela, and it occurred to him one night that she was as much a fixture as the stage she stood on. She was like the disco ball that spun near the ceiling, throwing light into the crowded darkness. One more expendable component of an endless night, her reflection ricocheting endlessly between mirrored walls. There were two other regular dancers there whom he'd been introduced to, Marie-Eve and Véronique, but to his eye they looked bored and stilted, no match for Michaela's loose-limbed extravagance. When the sound and the humanity got to be too much he pushed open the staff door, nodded at the bouncer who sat reading Dostoevsky just behind it, and made his way down to Michaela's dressing room. The building vibrated with dance music around him, and the pipes made strange noises. It was a little like being in the depths of a ship.

Her room wasn't large. There was a long counter with a sink, a chair beside a very small rickety table, and a clothing rack on wheels in the corner. Behind the clothing rack was a child-sized mattress, on which Michaela usually slept. It had a single sheet, a flat stained pillow, and an old quilt with little white sheep frolicking around the edges. He had a vision of Michaela as a very small child, lying under the sheep quilt in peaceful sleep, and on bad days the thought brought tears to his eyes. When he couldn't stand the crowd on the dance floor he went down to her dressing room and sat there for an hour, two hours, three, trying to concentrate on the idea of Lilia and thinking instead of Michaela on the stage until her stiletto footsteps sounded softly on the worn carpet outside, until the cheap door opened and she closed it behind her and sank into the chair by the makeup counter. It seemed to him that she had a way of absorbing the light when she came into a room. It didn't make her brilliant. She emanated a certain quality of darkness, clear and vivid, a kind of negative light.

"You didn't want to wait at the coffee shop?" she asked without looking at him.

"It's too cold to go up there. I've been walking all day. I wanted to make sure you had a place to stay tonight."

"Oh, it'll get colder. Have you seen my pills? Did Jacques bring them?"

"They're in the bag under the sink. Do you have a place to stay?"

She shrugged, not paying attention, pulling pill bottles from the paper bag that Jacques had brought and reading the labels. As far as Eli knew, she had no permanent address. She maintained a number of casual lovers and slept at their apartments sometimes. On other nights she slept in her dressing room. She was addicted to a complicated array of prescription medications, which the owner of the club helpfully provided. "He takes care of his assets" was all she'd say when asked about this odd arrangement, and she refused to elaborate. The owner, Jacques, came into her dressing room in the evenings with brown bags of pills from the pharmacy, cans of soda, greasy takeout food. She picked half-heartedly at the food and threw most of it away. Jacques was a tall, sad-eyed man with a seemingly limitless collection of silk shirts and a resigned expression. Around him Michaela was quiet, almost mute. She said *merci* when he gave her the pills and the food and the soda and said little else. Jacques carried himself with an air of long-suffering calm and said almost nothing himself. He didn't appear to have noticed Eli, which gave Eli the impression that he was far from the first guest to take up semi-residence in Michaela's dressing room, and then he spent hours and days wondering why he was upset by this.

"I wanted to offer," Eli said, "if you wanted to, you could stay in my hotel room. I'll sleep on the carpet."

"I don't stay in hotel rooms."

"I didn't mean it like that."

"It's okay." At length she selected two bottles from the paper bag that Jacques had brought her and swallowed a pill from each. "I have to go up to the VIP lounge in an hour anyway. I think I'll just sleep here tonight."

"Are you sure?"

"It's too cold to go outside."

He stood up awkwardly. "I'll meet you here tomorrow, then."

"Fine. Don't come till afternoon."

He stopped by the door. "Did Lilia used to wait for you like this?"

"Goodnight, Eli," Michaela said.

The cold outside felt like death to him. He walked as quickly as possible toward the hotel, composing a letter to Lilia in his head. *I want to find you. I want to disappear with you. I want to find you, and in the finding to make you disappear into me. I want to be your language. I want to be your translator. I want to be your dictionary. I want to be your map. I wish, I wish, I wish I knew where you are tonight.* In the hotel room he wrote all of this down on hotel stationery, crumpled it up, and threw it away. The words brought her no closer to him.

IN THE LATE AFTERNOON Michaela was worn and sleepy, a night creature blinking in the winter light. He met her at the side door of Club Electrolite and then had to wait while she ran back downstairs to get something she'd forgotten to put in her purse. He paced back and forth in the frozen alleyway, jumped up and down to try to unthaw his feet, did a few jumping jacks and had to stop because the cold hurt his lungs, finally knocked on the door again. Another dancer opened it.

"Véronique," he said, "I'm just waiting for Michaela. Could I wait inside?"

She had stringy blond hair and a suspicious way of looking at him, and he hadn't been sure in their previous meetings whether or not she spoke English. She hesitated. He shivered impatiently in the landscape of grimy ice.

"Okay," she said. She stepped back just enough to let him in and then stood looking at him in the dim hallway, at the top of the stairs leading down to the dressing room, and he felt absurdly compelled to make small talk.

"It's cold," he said.

"It gets colder."

"You've lived here all your life?" he asked.

She shook her head.

"From Chicoutimi," she said.

"Where's that?"

"North. Very north."

He nodded. "Even colder than here?"

"You like it here?" Véronique asked, perhaps not understanding.

"No."

She stared blankly at him for a moment.

"You wait outside," she said.

"Fine. Tell Michaela to hurry up."

The door closed behind him and he stood in the alleyway again. He kicked at an empty vodka bottle and it shattered instantly; he was staring at the broken glass when Michaela emerged. They walked a few blocks together down Rue Sainte-Catherine, retreated into Montreal's endless underground mall to escape the cold. She was pale and quiet, rubbing her wrists from time to time as they walked.

"I think the cruise ship's still there," she said suddenly. "I was thinking about going down there earlier." They had stopped at the foot of a low flight of stairs between malls. A cellist had set himself up on an overturned milk carton and was playing Bach's first cello suite. She was leaning against a wall, staring into space, and she had seemed so lost in the music that Eli was startled to hear her speak.

"Cruise ship?"

"There's supposed to be this colossal cruise ship down at the harbour. I read it in the paper earlier."

"Do you want to go see it?"

She shook her head. "I did. But it's so cold out there."

"How late did you work last night?"

"Five A.M.," she said. "Bachelor party in the VIP lounge."

"What kind of bachelor party?"

She gave him a look and started walking again. The cellist glanced up at her as they passed, and she smiled. "It's so beautiful," she said. "I hear music like this, and I understand why people love this place." The music was fading behind them. He'd been down here before with her, and he'd thought sometimes that the underground mall seemed to go on forever; an eternity of Gaps and stores that sold cell phones and wheeled carts that sold muffins, broken here and there by food courts. The same restaurants reappeared every few minutes. McDonald's, Sbarro, Wendy's, McDonald's. Lilia remained vanishing. There was Christmas music on the sound system, but turned down too low to make out which language the lyrics were in.

"I'm tired," she said. They stopped in a random food court, this one all white, and she sprawled loosely at a round white plastic table. She cut a strange figure in this pale underground place. Black platform boots and a silver jacket, short white hair standing on end. Red lipstick, grey eye shadow, startling green eyes. She looked drawn and sickly in the fluorescent light.

"Maybe it wouldn't be so bad," he said, "going to see the ship."

"It's so cold outside. Imagine what it's like down by the river."

He nodded and didn't speak for a while.

"My bed at home," he said, "it has a figurehead attached to it. Talking about ships always makes me think of it."

"Why does it have a figurehead?"

"I don't know, it just does. It's made out of a fishing boat, and my mother . . . Michaela, listen. I want to go home. Can you please just tell me where Lilia is."

She smiled without looking at him. She seemed peaceful at that moment, untroubled, looking far away. "Look, my position hasn't changed," she said. "I need to know about the accident." Michaela was rubbing her wrists again. She seemed to have returned from the VIP lounge with some mild rope burns.

"But you know where she is."

"I won't tell you where she is until you tell me about the accident. You know that."

Michaela and Eli lapsed into silence beneath the fabric leaves of a synthetic tree, and the Christmas music on the sound system was a film of white noise over the surface of the day. At this hour of the afternoon, the food court wasn't crowded. Passersby moved silently through a landscape of plastic tables and pale tiles, weighed down by their winter coats. A few of the other tables were occupied: blank-eyed office workers on lunch breaks ate greasy food from Styrofoam containers and stared into space. A pair of girls with Gap name tags picked at muffins and laughed nervously at a table nearby.

A food-court worker was cleaning tables. He gestured at a

tray on Michaela's table and said something to her; Eli watched her, waiting for her to respond, but she only looked at him. He repeated himself.

"*Je ne parle pas français,*" she said.

The man shook his head and retreated, the tray untouched.

"What did you just say to him?"

"I said, *I don't speak French.* It's a useful phrase around here."

"You don't speak French?"

"Not really. A few words. I never could. He could've just repeated himself in English."

"He might not speak English. How can you live here without speaking French?"

"Exactly," she said, still watching the food-court worker. "It wouldn't have mattered if they'd never left the circus."

He looked at her across the white plastic table, thinking of the couple who had laughed at him when he'd asked for directions in English on his first night in the city, and felt oddly that he was beginning to understand her.

OUTSIDE THE CAFÉ the cold deepened until the streets froze white. Michaela drank black tea at five in the morning, dazed with pills and insomnia but unable to sleep. Eli kept thinking that if he sat with her long enough, if she got tired enough in the small hours of the morning, if she kept talking and talking the way she did in this state, she'd slip; she'd say where Lilia was, where Lilia might be, if Lilia was still in this frozen city, if Lilia was even still alive, if Lilia had even ever actually existed in the first place, but instead she told him stories about terrorists and circuses.

"Did I ever tell you about the Second Cup bomber?"

"No," he said, "I don't think you did."

There had been a brief period during Michaela's adolescence when cafés with English names had had a tendency to detonate, which she seemed to think squared nicely with the general drama of her teenaged years. She'd taken to spending a great deal of time in cafés around that period, in the hope of being caught up in something dramatic and historic and great, but then the solitary lunatic had been caught and jailed before another one exploded. She seemed disappointed by this. He stared at her, unsure whether she was telling the truth, and she launched into another story about her grandparents' circus instead of telling him where Lilia was.

Her loneliness was like a third presence at the café table. They sat together by the hour, and both were aware that the moment he knew where Lilia was he would vanish back to New York and she'd be shipwrecked alone on the ice floe. She held her stories like currency and dispensed small change night by night. Notes on the circular qualities of obsession, like a snake tattoo biting its tail: the little girl scheming about dynamite and tightropes in her bedroom, the detective father obsessed with Lilia downstairs, the mother who brought home a cake and then disappeared forever. Michaela always had another story to tell him. Her stories were always in the margins of Lilia's life. She was always about to tell him where Lilia was. And he was usually only too happy to sit with her indefinitely and avoid the hotel with its painfully empty bed and deadpan bellboys, but he sometimes fell asleep in his café chair with his chin on his chest, arms folded, drifting off into cold dreams about exploding cafés and cake and tightropes. She stayed with him, ordered more tea at intervals, glared with bloodshot eyes at the arrival of morning. He fell asleep to the sound of her voice, and sometimes when he woke up she was still talking.

She talked about languages sometimes near morning. Specifically, what it was like to speak the wrong one in a place where the use of a particular language is enforced by means of a tip line for citizen informants. Laws were in place in the province of Quebec to ensure the usage of French, agencies were set up to enforce them, and a 1-800 number connected callers to La Commission de protection de la langue française to report violations. A violation could be as small as English appearing before French on a sign, she said, or the English appearing in larger letters, or a salesgirl saying *hello* instead of *bonjour* on a Sunday afternoon in the ladies' shoe department. Penalties included fines and the revocation of business licenses.

"Try to imagine," she said, "what it's like when you can't speak the right language in a place like this." She had been explaining a graffiti tag they'd walked by near Club Electrolite: *Montréal en français: 101 ou 401.* Bill 101 was one of the laws that specifically restricts the use of the English language. The 401 was the highway out of the city. *Speak French or get out.*

"I know," he said gently, "but did I ever tell you about my field of study?"

She went silent, noncommittal, tracing tightropish lines with one finger in the fog of a café windowpane. Outside the streets were achingly cold, and he felt it through the windows. Eli held his coffee mug with both hands to keep his fingers warm. It was almost four A.M.

"There are six thousand languages spoken on this earth," he said. "I told you that much, right?"

She wrote a slow, looping *6,000* in the windowpane fog without looking at him.

"And the thing is, almost all of them will disappear."

She seemed to like this idea. She smiled, stopped writing on the windowpane and sipped her newest cup of tea, gazed out the window at the huddled pedestrians, didn't speak again for quite a while. The thought of disappearing languages seemed to make her happy.

"I found a new alleyway the other day," she said finally. "Well, the same alleyway, but another spot farther down."

"The one where I met you?"

"No. A different one."

"I wish you wouldn't."

"Why not?"

"It's dangerous. Why do you walk on tightropes?"

"It's as close as I can get to all that . . ." And *all that*, at that moment in that café in that cold northern city, was the time that she could almost see and almost remember, genetic memory planted long before her birth. An imagined life spent travelling through small towns with lions and tents and tightropes and sideshows, a long line of trailers winding down the highway between fields and trees, sunlight glinting on windshields; setting up tents in the field, the parking lot, the smell of popcorn and candy apples.

"You've travelled?" she asked.

"A little. Yes. I've been to Europe a few times with my brother. Spain, Paris, Eastern Europe, Turkey, one time we travelled around a bit in southern Italy."

"The time with the boat?"

"I told you about that trip?"

"No, Lilia did."

"Oh," he said. "Yes. The time with the boat. She liked that story. We were fishing for squids."

"Did you catch any?"

"No."

"I dated a guy once," she said, "who'd travelled around Europe a lot, and he said eventually everywhere seemed kind of interchangeable. Is it like that? When you travel, do all the places seem the same?"

How deep in our genes is the longing for flight embedded? We always were a species of nomads. Eli found it easy to imagine an instinct passed down generation to generation, a permanently thrown breaker on a genetic switchboard: *flight or fight*, and a switch jammed permanently in the *flight* position, the limitless longing for travel pulled down by hooked genes. It leapfrogs a generation (she said her parents had wanted to be a detective and a real estate agent, even when they were kids), and is thwarted when it reappears. She leaned across the table, asked him if it was true that all places look the same, and the least unkind thing he could do at that moment was nod and lie to her. *Yes. It's true. I have been to half a dozen countries, and all the world looks the same to me.* He thought it would be unimaginably cruel to tell her that all of the individual places she hadn't seen were different.

"I don't believe you," she answered, settling back in her chair, the moment passed.

30

In the spring when Lilia was fifteen she was travelling north out of Florida. It had been two years since the *Unsolved Cases* feature, and her life was played out in a shifting, paranoid landscape: abandoned meals on restaurant tables, impressions of figures passing just out of sight, an old blue car with Quebec licence plates that she saw three times in different places, a constant feeling of being watched from behind.

There was no sense in talking about it. At some point that year, she had stopped hiding in the back of the car. She was getting too big to comfortably disappear into the backseat of an automobile anyway, and there was a feeling of waiting for something inevitable to occur. Her father was moving her faster and faster from place to place. By that frenzied summer they were in a different motel room every night. Sometimes they'd check into one motel, pay for two nights, and then drive to another a few miles away. Sometimes they'd sleep through the day and then drive all through the night, speaking softly or sitting together in silence, listening to night radio, hypnotized by headlights, three A.M. meals in the hallucinogenic glare of open-all-night restaurants on the interstate, going to bed near morning in a cheap motel with parking around back. She dyed her hair at least every month, from blond to dark brown and back again, across entire spectrums of auburns and reds, forever covering the trail. Lilia's hair felt dry and soft to the touch, and her scalp was always itchy. She spent an hour at a time in the motel shower, soothed by the water, massaging conditioner into her head. She wore dark glasses during the daytime, a baseball cap pulled down low. She met no one's eyes in public. She wanted gazes to pass over her without stopping. She wanted to be forgotten.

That was the spring she crossed into Arizona for the one hundredth time and had her first glass of red wine to celebrate. It was possibly the worst thing she'd ever tasted, but her father told her that all the best tastes in life are acquired, and she liked the way the liquid in the glass caught the light. That night her father woke her at two in the morning, not for any reason that he could articulate, and they were gone by two-twenty. On the highway she tried to go back to sleep, but couldn't. She sat awake, wired and anxious, into the morning and all through the afternoon, until finally on the other side of the state her father pulled into the parking lot of the Stillspell Motel. She had a dull pounding headache from sleeplessness and the half glass of wine.

"Here," he said. "I can't drive anymore. Let's get some rest." He was haggard in the sunlight, hollow-eyed. In the motel room he went to bed and slept for three hours while Lilia read newsmagazines at the fake-wood table in the lamplight. He was breathing almost silently. She kept reading the same paragraph over and over, looking over at him in the dimness to make sure she could still see his chest moving. She had never been so tired, but when she lay on the other bed a few feet away from him, there was a strange feeling of responsibility. For the first time in her life, she felt that she had to stay awake so he could sleep. Three or four cars pulled into the parking lot, and every single time she went to the window, but none of them were the blue car with foreign licence plates. After a while she got out her camera and stood by the window taking photographs of the parking lot in the late-afternoon light to calm herself.

"You don't need to keep watch," he said.

"I thought you were asleep."

He was sitting up and pulling his boots on. Smiling the way he used to, before they were travelling to a new town every night.

"I was," he said. "But you still don't have to watch over me."

They walked out together into the warm May afternoon. The Stillspell Motel faced the highway. It was flanked on either side by the Morning Star Diner and Stillspell Auto Repair, and the three buildings (all low-slung, old, and in need of renovations) formed a decrepit open horseshoe facing away from the town. Or if not a horseshoe, perhaps a stage: three buildings at right angles and a parking lot between them, the highway blank and grey along the invisible fourth wall. Across the highway was a landscape of chaparral that seemed more or less infinite.

"Where are we?" Lilia asked.

"Town of Stillspell, apparently."

"I meant which state."

"Arizona. No. Wait. New Mexico. I'm almost sure we're in New Mexico."

"New Mexico," the waitress in the Morning Star Diner confirmed brightly. She liked Stillspell, she said, although she did think sometimes about leaving. When she'd brought the food she installed herself not far from them, leaning on the side of a banquette, while Lilia slumped over her chocolate milkshake and tried to remember her current name. She hadn't slept in far too long, and it was getting on into the evening. There weren't that many people left here, the waitress said. The population had dropped so low that it couldn't really be considered a town anymore. There was virtually no work here. It was almost a ghost village. But she had a job and a house, and she thought she might stay awhile. She'd never really left, except when she was young and had run away with her boyfriend to Phoenix. But Phoenix was so big, and people weren't friendly to her, and fourteen's a bit young for that kind of thing, actually, and would they like some more coffee?

"No," said Lilia's father. "Thank you. But I'd be curious to know your name."

"Clara," said the waitress. "A pleasure."

"Likewise," he said, and gave her a fake name that Lilia immediately forgot.

"Are you staying long?"

"Oh, a day or two maybe," her father said, "just to rest up a little. We've been travelling cross-country, Allie and I."

"Allie," said the waitress. "What's that short for?"

"Alessandra," Lilia said, and flashed an exhausted smile.

"Alessandra," the waitress repeated. She flicked a strand of hair behind her left ear. Her hair was straight and red and went to her shoulders, and she had china-blue eyes. She liked the name: "Alessandra," she said again. "Spanish, right?"

Lilia was tired, and the details of the night grew hazy. Her father and the waitress were talking about music. Lilia was falling asleep at the table. Her father and Clara were talking for what seemed like a long time; later on she couldn't remember how it had been decided that they'd be staying at Clara's house that night instead of, say, in their paid-for room in the Stillspell Motel, but she found herself walking with Clara and her father down a cracked street in the moonlight, old houses silent on either side. A dog was barking in the distance. Some windows were lit up, while others stood unlit. There were a few stores with boards over the windows.

Clara had a house like an optical illusion. A glance around the living room revealed her singular interests: she liked shoes, and the ocean, and things that flew. A dozen sets of stilettos were lined up at attention along one wall in the living room. The walls had pictures of winged things, hummingbirds and pterodactyls and rickety-looking antique airplanes. The house, in the meantime, left no doubt as to her vast and final passion. Every wall, every ceiling, every surface was blue. There were watercolour fishes swimming up the staircase. She told Lilia much later that she was happy never having seen a real ocean. She was afraid it wouldn't live up to her expectations.

She'd hung blue silk curtains over the living room windows and they rippled, water-like, in the breeze of a fan. There was a fish mobile hanging from the ceiling. The house was old and big—her grandfather had bought it for a song, she said, a few years after the mine had closed, back when everyone was leaving all at once. Lilia pictured an old man standing in the desert singing, open and pleading with eyes as blue as Clara's. Clara insisted on an immediate tour of the kingdom: later Lilia remembered trailing after them through stranger and stranger rooms, until she asked to take a bath and was left with towels and a bathrobe in the upstairs bathroom.

Lilia lay almost floating in the claw-footed bathtub, the water around her deep and green and still. There were extravagant fish painted freehand on the walls, intensely brilliant creatures of pure colour, pure light, with watercolour-green seaweed floating between them in the deep. There was a rubber fish toy on a tiled shelf by the bathtub, smiling next to a yellow rubber duck. She lay still in the water for a long time, listening to the steady dripping of the tap. Her father and Clara were somewhere distant in the house. Their voices and laughter floated up the stairs.

In the morning Lilia woke in an upstairs guest bedroom. There were old-looking toy airplanes suspended from the ceiling above her head. Her father and Clara were up already, drinking coffee. Later, her father left Lilia with Clara and a stack of pancakes and walked back to the motel to get the car and the luggage.

"Someone came by looking for you the other night," the desk clerk said helpfully.

"What?"

"Here, he left me his card." The desk clerk dug around in the receipts for a moment and produced a plain white card with neat black type: *Christopher Graydon, Private Investigator*, an address in Montreal.

"Did he say anything?"

"Just that he was looking for you. He said he needed to speak with you as soon as possible."

"Is he still here?" Lilia's father asked.

"He left this morning."

"He hasn't been back?"

"No. He went off down the highway."

"Which way did he go?"

The man stared curiously at him for a moment. "Well, I guess it was east," he said.

The door to the motel room was swinging open. The room was subtly altered. Lilia's father stood looking in, and it took a moment to see the disturbance that he sensed: a Bible was open on the bed, with a page ripped out. He didn't know about Lilia's habit of leaving messages and so didn't understand why this was. What he did understand was that someone had been here. He stood for a while on the threshold, the detective's business card in his pocket, and realized that they'd been saved the night before. It was never possible for him to look at Clara afterward without imagining that she was in some way protective, in some way divine, a patron saint of fugitives in a roadside café. He decided to stop travelling and stay by her side.

31

"Did you find her?" the bellboy asked.

It was early afternoon, and Eli had woken up only recently. He hadn't noticed the bellboy board the elevator. He looked up, blinking, and remembered being given directions to Club Electrolite on his first night in the city.

"The girl you're looking for," the bellboy said.

"No. Not yet."

"Where have you been looking?" the bellboy asked, just before the doors opened into the lobby.

"Everywhere," Eli said.

In the afternoons he walked through Montreal with a map of the city folded up small in his jacket pocket. He walked for miles, moved in and out of the subway system, tried to look at everyone he could in case they might be Lilia. It was an effort to keep his head up, to look into the faces of passersby. His eyes watered from the cold and then his eyelashes froze, and he was forever blinking against the winter light. In the old city he walked the narrow streets along the waterfront, stepping into a café every time he lost feeling in his feet. He left the first footsteps in pristine snow in the deserted parks. He lingered in English bookstores in Westmount and French bookstores in Mile End, on the theory that Lilia might buy books in either language and might be just as desperate to escape the cold as he was. Downtown he found a building that he thought Lilia might like, and he returned again and again, at first just in case she arrived to photograph it, and later on because it moved him. It was an old and very narrow building, three storeys high and surrounded on three sides by a cracked parking lot, and it had been transformed almost entirely into an anime cartoon: on the east side was a woman screaming, with dark purple hair and furious pale-blue eyes. Her face took up the entire side of the building. On the west side a man stared west, blond and suspicious and narrow-eyed, partially obscured by a billboard advertising Cuban vacations, but it was the screaming woman who held Eli's attention. She was screaming in fury, he realized, not fear. There could be no doubt when he studied her eyes. Eli couldn't stand out in the street for very long in the cold, but he returned to the cartoon building over and over again, wishing he was a photographer, standing on nearby corners and looking up at it. The painted woman screamed out over the city, east toward the low brick apartment blocks of Centre-Sud, over the alleyways turned by graffiti artists into dark beautiful murals, over the dilapidated houses with their spiral staircases and strange turrets, the endless porn theatres and strip clubs, the people who walked on frozen sidewalks with their hands in their pockets and their breath turning to ice inside their scarves. She seemed like the only passionate thing in the landscape, and her fury gave him a kind of hope.

He came down to Michaela's dressing room in the evenings and lay on his back on the carpet, or sat on the chair by the table behind her while she prepared herself for the night, reading the English papers, studying his map. Sometimes he stretched out on the floor and fell asleep while she was performing. He seemed to have fallen into limitless exhaustion. It was always possible for him to fall asleep. He had dreams about ice cubes. He was almost always cold. Once he woke up and she'd turned off the lights in the room. A candle flickered between them on the carpet, melting onto a grimy plate. She was lying on the other side of the candle, still dressed in tight vinyl, her hands over her eyes. The room smelled of hairspray and candle smoke.

"What time is it?"

She turned her head to look at him. "Three A.M.," she said. "You're awake."

"Barely." His neck was stiff. "You'll burn this place down."

"It's on a plate, Eli. Did you ever read about the Gnostics?"

He sat up slowly, looking at her. Her face was barely visible in the dimness.

"Yes," he said. "How many pills have you taken?"

"Lilia used to talk about them."

"The pills?"

"The Gnostics. She never talked about them with you?"

"Maybe once," he lied, obscurely jealous. Michaela smiled.

"They appeared seventeen years after the death of Jesus Christ. She talked about these stories. *Prophets walking the streets of Jerusalem*, her words, not mine . . ."

"They're not her words," he said. "They're from a book I own. I didn't know she read it."

"Anyway, I like them. The Gnostics believed that none of this is real," she said. "None of this seems real to me."

"It's the pills," he said.

"No, it's everything. This life, these pills, Club Electrolite, this dressing room. How could there be a city like this in the world? How could it possibly be so cold? What I mean is that every light is too bright for me. Every sound is too loud."

"It's late," he said quietly. "You must be exhausted. You should go to sleep."

Her eyes were shining. "You move like a ghost over the surface of the world," she said. "Am I right?"

He realized that she was talking about him specifically, and also that she was somewhat more unhinged than usual, and said, "I'm not sure."

"The thing is," she said, sitting upright and holding her knees to her chest, "the thing is, I can't sleep anymore. Days go by sometimes if I don't send myself to sleep with all these white little pills. And I used to think I could find some kind of peace in this city. I had a job that I liked . . ." Eli propped himself up on one elbow to watch her face in the guttering candlelight. Her voice was somnambulant.

She talked on through the night, while Eli listened and eventually fell asleep again on the carpet, and her voice was a current through fitful dreams. When he woke she was still talking, lying on her back, and the candle was drowning in a pool of wax. There were no windows here, no natural light to give a clue as to the hour of the night, of the morning, but he had a sense of having been asleep for some time. She was mumbling, whispering, and he couldn't understand her.

"Michaela." She fell silent and turned her head to look at him. There was a cold draft from somewhere and he couldn't keep his eyes open. His throat was dry. "What time is it?"

She sat up slowly, fumbled in the darkness for her purse. After a moment she extracted her cell phone, and her face was lit blue for a moment when she looked at the screen.

"It's six-thirty," she said. "No, six-thirty-five. I've been awake for two days." She put her cell phone back in her bag and sat there with her legs outstretched on the carpet in front of her, slumped over and looking at her hands, shaking her head, a ghost in the half-light. She was barefoot.

"Do you have any sleeping pills?"

She nodded and gestured toward the purse. He thought perhaps she was crying, but it was impossible to tell. The candle was a flicker of blue in a pool of melted wax. He could barely make out her face.

"What's the worst thing you could imagine happening?" she asked suddenly. She was watching his struggle with the childproof cap.

"I don't know. I'm too tired for rhetorical questions."

"It's not rhetorical, it's theoretical. There's a difference." Her voice cracked, and she coughed once. "My throat's dry."

"I'll get you some water. What's the worst thing *you* could imagine?" He succeeded in opening the cap and measured three white dots into the palm of his hand. He rose and moved stiffly to the counter. It took a minute to find the glass he'd seen there earlier. The tap gurgled invisibly in the darkness. He held his hand under the cold water until he began losing feeling in his fingertips and then touched his wet fingertips lightly to his forehead before he returned to her. A trick Zed had taught him; the cold water on his forehead made him feel more awake.

"Never falling asleep again. Now tell me yours."

He knelt beside her on the carpet and touched her wrist. He placed the pills in her hand.

"Take these. I have some water for you."

"I need the water first," Michaela said. "Tell me yours."

"Here's the water."

"Tell me."

"I hate being alone." He took a sip of water and passed her the glass. She drank almost all of it and swallowed all three pills at once. "Where's Lilia tonight?" He spoke very softly.

"Close," she said. "She's very close." She finished the glass of water, set it down empty on the carpet, and then lay down beside it. She turned over on her side toward the candle, away from him. He stayed beside her.

"What would change if you knew about the accident? What difference would it make?"

"I just want to know," she said. "I want to know what happened to my family. My father disappeared earlier this year, did I tell you that? He sold the house and left, and I don't know where he is anymore. You never expect both of your parents to just *vanish* like that. It's a missing piece."

"But what happens when you have the final missing piece? Are you happy then? Can you stop taking pills? Do you stop entertaining bachelor parties in the VIP lounge on weekends? Does the knowledge solve anything?"

"Then maybe I can sleep," she said. She closed her eyes. "Please don't raise your voice."

"I'm sorry."

"Will you stay with me a minute?"

"Of course."

He stayed beside her until her breathing slowed, then he stood and groped in the dimness for the clothing rack. Under it, behind it, the sheep quilt was crumpled on the child-sized mattress. He pulled the quilt out and spread it over her, blew out the candle, and felt his way out of the room in absolute darkness.

32

In a small town in New Mexico, more of a truck stop really, a detective wearing a battered fedora sat in a car in a parking lot. He was watching a particular couple emerge from the Morning Star Diner: a man he'd been following for some years, and a waitress. The man was forty-seven years old that year, according to Christopher's records. He had a benevolent, somewhat weathered look, and brown hair that fell just below his ears. The woman was younger, with straight red hair and an old-fashioned blue-and-white waitressing uniform. She was holding a square white box. The detective remembered that it was Lilia's sixteenth birthday tomorrow and decided that Clara must be holding her birthday cake.

They paused for a moment outside the diner, the man pulled the waitress close against him, and they kissed briefly in the warm end-of-day light. The detective slowly lowered his forehead to rest on the steering wheel and stayed that way for some time with his eyes closed. He had been following them for five years now, but he was no longer sure why. The helpless observer: everyone knows that Icarus fell into the sea. But only one book he'd ever read on the subject remarked on the possible existence of witnesses: wandering with his flock on a hillside not far from the ocean, a shepherd looked up in time to watch the disastrous, improbable flight—the at-first-awkward beating of wings as the child and the father moved over the face of the water, the small shape that grew exultantly smaller as it flew closer and closer to the sun, until Icarus was so far away that the shepherd could no longer see him, only knew where he was from the way the father kept looking anxiously up into the sky, and then the scream from an almost unfathomable distance above, the fall, the coming apart of wax and feathers, that fast awful descent into the sea, the father moving down through the air to catch his child, too late. The cloud of feathers drifting up as Icarus broke the surface of the water, and the father circling desperately in the beaten air overhead. The shepherd, watching all of this from a slight distance, leaning on his staff while his sheep scattered like clouds. Awestruck, stunned, perhaps already composing the story he'd tell his wife that evening in his head, but at ease in the often uncomfortable awareness of being an extraneous figure in a world-historical event. His only part in the story: to observe and remember the chain of events. Not all of us will be cast in the greatest dramas. Someone has to remember them.

Or perhaps it's just this: memory is too unreliable to entrust a story to the hero alone. Someone else has to have observed the chain of events to lend credibility; if no one else remembers your story, how are you to prove that it was real? The witness, the man in the car in the parking lot told himself miserably, is not unimportant. (The couple was walking away from him now, toward Clara's house.) He had been travelling alone for thousands of miles, and the only thing he was at all certain of at that moment was that he didn't want to catch them anymore. He only wanted to watch their flight. Christopher raised his head from the steering wheel, rubbed his face with his hands, and decided that he needed to talk to Clara.

Two thousand miles to the north in another country, Michaela was sitting alone in her room. She was smoking fitfully, looking out the window. She had just turned sixteen, and she'd stopped going to school to celebrate. While she waited for her father to come back to her (she hadn't seen him in a year), she began taking walks to the Old Montreal alleyways on weekends with a measuring tape. She had wished her whole life for a chance to walk on a high wire without a safety net. She had ideas involving alleyways and lengths of rope.

33

Clara in the mornings: she descended the stairs in a bath-robe, yawning, the stairs creaking under her feet. In the kitchen she always opened the back door and stood for a moment looking out. She lived on the edge of town, and all the backyards on her side of the street opened out into the desert, a landscape of cacti and dry grass and scrubby blue-grey sagebrush that kept going until it met the hazy outlines of the mountains far away. The collapsed wreckage of an ancient picket fence marked a rectangle behind the house, but the lawn had been overtaken two decades before by the desert.

She came away from the door to begin making coffee. Lilia watched her from the kitchen table. She liked to sit there in the mornings, partly to read in the warm kitchen light and mostly to drink coffee with Clara. Clara poured coffee beans into an ancient cast-iron grinder mounted on the wall, measuring by eye, and then turned the iron handle until the smell of ground coffee filled the room. On the rare mornings when Lilia slept later than Clara, this was the sound that woke her up. Clara was moving efficiently in and out of cupboards, removing mugs and the coffee pot, she was boiling water on the stove. She used cloth filters in a battered plastic funnel the colour of sand. She poured boiling water until the clear glass coffee pot was almost full and then poured the coffee into the biggest mug in the house. She stood at the counter, sipping it black, and then she poured a second cup for Lilia, this one with milk in it. It was only after she'd brought the mugs to the table and sat in the chair closest to the back door, only after she'd taken another look out at the beautifully degenerate back lawn and the sky overhead, only then was she prepared to wish Lilia good morning, to have her first conversation of the day. She would smile companionably at Lilia before that moment, but her solitude before her first cup of coffee was almost impenetrable.

Lilia wrote in her notebook: *This is life in a house.* Clara had never travelled, and was perfectly serene. She'd lived alone for years in her small desert town and enjoyed her independence, although now her face lit up when Lilia's father entered the room.

When Lilia's father was with Clara he no longer looked like he was being chased, and Lilia was old enough to recognize this as happiness, but she was already moving away again. She was almost sixteen, and increasingly restless. She had had the same name for months now: *Alessandra.* The name was beautiful, but it wasn't hers. She loved her father, she adored Clara, she was desperate to leave. She walked for hours along the streets of this dusty outpost, she wandered out into the desert behind the house, she read endlessly and translated literature in and out of four languages, she lay awake at night and felt enclosed in the silent house. She had been thinking lately about travelling away on her own. But at that moment the kitchen was cool and pleasant and she was happy to be there, and Clara stood with her back to the kitchen table looking out the window above the kitchen sink, sipping her coffee for a moment before she brought Lilia a cup. She set the coffee down on the table in front of her, kissed Lilia unexpectedly on the forehead, smiled as she moved around the table to her favourite chair.

"Happy birthday," she said. "I'll bring home a cake tonight."

In the evening Lilia's father and Clara sang "Happy Birthday," her father's arm over Clara's shoulders, and Clara pulled a cake triumphantly from a square white box. The cake was white, with *Sweet 16* across the top in pink icing. Later the three of them climbed out Lilia's bedroom window to look at stars from the rooftop.

"It's hard to imagine a place much quieter than this," her father said. There was a dog barking somewhere far away, sporadically, but it only deepened the surrounding silence. Lilia held her hand up white against the stars and had the feeling of floating in space.

"It's why I stay here," Clara said.

"Are you ever going to leave?" Lilia asked.

Clara was quiet for a moment. "No. I mean, who can predict the future, but I don't think so. I left a couple of times before, and I didn't like it. Everywhere else was so . . . loud," she said. "It was too loud out there, in every way. The people weren't nice. No one knew my name. I didn't like it. I don't like travelling."

They had been in Stillspell for five months and the next day they were leaving. Just for four days, one last little birthday road trip for old times' sake, and then they were coming back to Stillspell forever. *Forever* is the most dizzying word in the English language. The idea of staying in one place forever was like standing at the border of a foreign country, peering over the fence and trying to imagine what life might be like on the other side, and life on the other side was frankly unimaginable. They left in the morning. Her father's car pulled out of Clara's driveway with the suitcases in the back, Clara waving from the porch. Lilia waved out the window until she was certain Clara couldn't see her anymore, the car turning behind a row of decrepit storefronts at the end of the street, and then she settled back in the passenger seat with a guilty sense of rhythm restored.

"Where should we go, my lily?"

"The desert for a day or two. Then the mountains."

"Brilliant plan." He nodded toward the map folded on the dashboard. "What's our course?"

Lilia took the map in her hands, marked with red lines drawn over the past nine years in motel rooms all around the continent, faded from nine summers of sun through the windshield. "Hard to say," she said.

"Aren't you supposed to be the navigator?"

"I know, I know, but look how faded this map is . . ."

He glanced at it and laughed. "We should hang this one in the house," he said, "and buy a new one for the road."

Clara was turning to go back into the house when she saw another car approaching; this one was blue, and had foreign licence plates. It pulled into her driveway as Lilia's father's car was turning out of sight. Clara stood by the door, obscurely afraid. A neighbour was trimming and trimming and trimming the adjoining hedge.

The man who emerged from the car was tall and stoop-shouldered, and he held a hat in front of his rumpled suit. He smiled as he approached her, but she didn't smile back.

"Clara Williams?"

She nodded and glanced at the neighbour, who met her eyes above the hedge and then looked away quickly.

"My name is Christopher Graydon. I'm a private investigator. I'd like to ask you a few questions."

"Not here," she said.

34

Michaela's father returned from the United States in a wheel-chair. He spent hours staring out the window in the living room, blinking and sometimes shaking his head. Private nurses came and went. His car had gone sideways off a high-way in the mountains, he said. When pressed he was able to give the date of the accident, but he was vague on the ques-tion of how exactly it had occurred. He said he might have fallen asleep at the wheel. Over the next two years he began walking on crutches, and then with a cane, stiffly, dragging one leg, not at all like the way he had walked before. He was given light assignments by the private investigative agency, mostly photographing cheating spouses from cars, and he drew a small pension from his years on the police force.

There was no more talk of Lilia's case. He told Peter the trail had gone cold. Peter reported that Lilia's mother had screamed at him and threatened to sue. But in the few years that followed, Christopher used to disappear for a few days at a time, travelling back into the States whenever he could. Just a long weekend sometimes, driving from Friday to Monday and arriving at work on Tuesday exhausted and worn. He had decided before the accident not to chase them anymore, but the circumstances of the accident made him fear for Lilia's safety. He would never bring her in, not anymore; all he wanted now was to watch over her. Michaela had been reading his notes for years, but his notes were only part of it. The other part was the way he woke up at night in his bed in Montreal and knew where Lilia was, the way he could glance at a map of the United States and realize with absolute, inexplicable certainty that she was in West Virginia, the way he tried to ignore his terrifying clairvoyance and forget where she was and couldn't, the way he knew where she was but had to keep driving south to check, the horror of always being right: he saw her face in the crowd on Sunset Boulevard, he stepped into a hardware store in St. Louis at the moment she stepped out of the deli across the street, he stood on a corner in a run-down neighbourhood in Chicago and watched her emerge from an apartment building down the block. After each sighting he returned north more depleted, more frightened, less intact.

The last time Michaela saw him was in the evening, when he'd just returned from the United States. She'd lost her job earlier in the day. In the years since she'd left high school she'd fallen into a pleasant double life. She worked at a clothing store five days a week and walked on ferociously dangerous tightropes strung across alleyways in the old city on weekends. But her manager had fired her in the early afternoon for speaking the wrong language on the sales floor, walked her to the door, shaken her hand when they got to the street. "Good luck," he'd said brightly, as if she were a needy stranger to whom he'd given a quarter, as though he hadn't just put her out of a job. "I hope things go well for you."

"I hope you die," Michaela said sweetly. She turned away from his aghast expression and soundlessly moving lips and wandered down the street in the cool September light, hands in her pockets and shaking inside, and the store receded instantly into the distant past; it seemed inconceivable that she'd gone to work there just that morning. It seemed inconceivable that she'd been living a life so ordinary for so long now, so long, living in her father's house in the almost-suburb of Westmount and folding clothes for a living. People were talking and laughing and the leaves on the trees hadn't fallen yet. The air was bright. A little girl was playing a violin at the corner of Sainte-Catherine and McGill; she was no older than ten, and her face was a vision of impeccable serenity. Michaela stood watching her face for a while, but she couldn't hear the music above the din of her thoughts. A band of tourists passed, speaking English, and only then did she notice that everyone else walking past her was speaking French. It struck her that she'd rarely been so lonely, or so incompatible with the world, or so strange. She spent some time in the park and arrived home after nightfall, slightly drunk.

The newspapers had been collected from the front step. The front-step newspapers were a private marker. She let them pile up in the weeks when her father was travelling, and when they disappeared it meant he was home and she knew what to expect when she opened the front door. When she came in this evening, her father was eating dinner in the dining room. He looked up and smiled briefly as she walked into the room; she sank into a chair across the table from him and sat watching him eat for a moment.

"Where did you go this time?"

He swallowed, and took a sip of water before he answered. "Chicago," he said.

"Chicago."

"Yes." He swallowed another spoonful of soup and took a bite of bread. "I was following a lead."

"You were following Lilia."

There was an uncomfortable pause, during which he finished his bread, sipped at his water again, and set the glass back down on the table with exaggerated restraint.

"Well," he said, "I suppose that's one way of looking at it, yes. I was interviewing a girl who knew her there."

"What was her name?"

"Erica."

"What was she like?"

He hesitated a moment. "She was sad," he said. "She had blue hair. How was your day?"

"I lost my job."

"At the clothing store? I'm sorry," he said. "You were laid off? Business was slow?"

"Fired, actually. I said hello to a little kid on the sales floor. His mother complained to the manager."

"Why would she complain to the manager? That doesn't make any sense."

"It makes perfect sense," said Michaela. "I said hello in English."

"Oh," he said.

"She felt quite strongly about the issue, apparently."

"Zealots," said Christopher. He shook his head. "You just have to ignore them. What did your manager say?" It occurred to him that this was the most substantial conversation he could remember having with his daughter in years, and he tried not to look pleased.

"He was regretful. Said she'd told him she was going to call the language commission, said he liked me but we'd been through this before and he couldn't afford to be fined by the language police again, hoped I understood, but I don't."

"Don't what?"

"Understand. I don't understand this place. I liked working there."

"Well. I don't think it's right either. But maybe there's a chance of getting your job back in a week or two, once he calms down a little. How did you leave off with him?"

"I told him to drop dead," said Michaela.

He wasn't sure he'd heard her correctly. There was a certain look about her eyes that reminded him of her mother. He dipped a piece of bread in his soup and ate without looking at her.

"Listen," he said, "I've got some news of my own. I'm selling the house. An appraiser's coming by tomorrow."

"What? Why?"

"I need the money," Christopher said, "to be honest with you."

"You have a job."

"I do," he said. "Photographing people from cars, mostly. But I want to do some travelling, so I'm going to have to leave the job for a while."

"Don't you have savings?" she asked.

"I did," he said.

"But where will we live?"

"Well," he said, "I'll be travelling. And you, well, I thought maybe you might want to find your own place one of these days. Have a little independence, maybe live closer to downtown?"

"But I just lost my job."

He had nothing to say to this.

"By travelling," she said, "you mean following Lilia?"

"Yes. It's an open case."

"There isn't a retainer? You said once there's always a retainer when you're following someone."

"It ran out a while ago. The contract expired."

"There's something that I don't quite understand," she said.

He glanced up briefly, and then down at his soup. She was making him uneasy. He reached out with his left hand and his fingertips passed nervously over the smooth handle of his walking cane, leaning against the table by his side.

"What's that?" He lifted the glass of water a few inches, changed his mind, lowered it to the table again, and adjusted his napkin on his lap.

"Why you're still following her."

"She's an abducted child," he said. "That's what I *do*."

"An abducted child? Do you know how old she is?"

He swallowed a spoonful of soup and chased it with a sip of water. He set the glass down on the table and then, with a thumb and two fingers, moved it carefully an inch to the left.

"Of course I know how old she is," he said quietly. He didn't lift his gaze from the glass. "I know almost everything about her."

"She's two months older than I am. Do you know how old I am?"

A spoonful of soup was halfway to his mouth. He lowered it back into the bowl and touched a corner of napkin to his lips.

"You're my daughter," he said.

"It seems very strange to me," Michaela continued, very quietly now, "that you would chase a twenty-two-year-old woman to Chicago. She was abducted quite some time ago, wasn't she?"

"Don't," he whispered. He wanted to explain it to her: the cufflink he'd found on the floor that morning, that tie on the floor of the closet, the way Elaine had sometimes looked at him when he got into bed at night, with such *contempt*, as if he couldn't find a lost sock, let alone a missing child, but it came to him suddenly that it was years too late.

"You've been chasing her since we were both eleven years old," said Michaela relentlessly. She felt giddy and dangerous, slightly drunk, and she couldn't stop talking although she knew she should. "And now she isn't a child anymore. Not that that negates the crime, but then, if you were trying to solve the crime, you'd be chasing her father, wouldn't you?"

He didn't speak. A muscle in his jaw worked uselessly, and his face was slowly turning red.

"You'd be chasing Lilia's father," she said, "except that you're obsessed with Lilia. And I wish you'd just admit it."

"Admit what?" His voice was a croak.

"That you want to fuck her," Michaela said.

It would have been difficult to predict what happened

next. He had, after all, never even hit her. But then the glass in his hand was abruptly airborne, almost of its own volition; he couldn't remember deciding to throw it. He watched the trajectory unfold in slow motion, the girl in the gradually-becoming-clearer line of flight, the intersection of her forehead with the edge of the glass, her backward fall, the sound she made. His cane was in his hand, although he couldn't remember having reached for it. He made his way around the table and saw her lying still and white in the overturned chair. There was blood on her forehead. He was aware in that instant of nothing but colour and light: the deep-blue evening behind his ghostly reflection in the dining room windows, and fragments of light from the chandelier caught in the broken angles of glass, spilled water. He had shocked himself. He reeled backward, touched the wall with his hand and slid down it. The room was moving like a boat on rough water.

Michaela was staggering to her feet, bleeding from the forehead, backing up and clutching the table. She swore softly and spat at his feet. She left the room like a sleepwalker, leaning to the right. The door slammed. He heard her fall once on the gravel outside, her receding stumbling footsteps, and then silence. The room had stopped spinning in her absence, but everything was too bright. He sat still for a long time, looking at the way light caught in the angles of broken glass and spilled water and along the glinting handle of her soup spoon, on the varnish of her chair lying on its back, in a smear of blood on the hardwood where she'd fallen.

"I'm sorry," he said. He wasn't sure if he was talking to himself or to his ex-wife. Lately he'd found himself talking to Michaela's mother when he was alone, but talking to a previous version, the old Elaine, the circus Elaine who hadn't disappeared yet, before they were detective and real estate agent and before Michaela was even born, playing on the midway before the show opened, riding together in the house trailer from town to town and looking out the windows at the prairie passing by, holding hands in the shadows behind the tent. It hadn't really been so bad in retrospect, travelling around like that. He stood up unsteadily and returned very slowly to his side of the table, leaning heavily on the cane as he sank into the chair and lifted his spoon. He found himself looking at the spoon for several long minutes, almost unsure what to do with it, but he eventually resumed eating his soup.

35

Erica was outside Lilia's apartment in the morning. The last morning, the day Lilia left Chicago. She stepped out with her suitcase and Erica was there on the sidewalk, blue-haired and shivering in an old velvet smoking jacket the colour of peaches. She was leaning against the side of the building, staring at her feet, or perhaps her eyes were closed—her hair fell over her face—and Lilia had the impression that she'd been standing there for some time. The lines of her shoulders spoke of exhaustion and night.

Lilia said her name, and she looked up quickly with swollen eyes.

"It's so early, Erica, what are you—"

"I don't want you to leave."

Lilia set down her suitcase. Erica took a cautious step toward her, stumbled forward and was suddenly in Lilia's arms. She was wearing perfume. She smelled like roses and cigarettes.

"Erica," Lilia whispered into her blue hair, "Erica, I'm so sorry, I really am . . ."

"What's in New York City?" Erica's voice was muffled against Lilia's shoulder. "Why won't you stay with me? You don't know *anyone* there."

"I'm so sorry, but I have to go." Erica's shoulders were shaking now. Lilia held her awkwardly. "You knew I wasn't staying here long when you met me." Her own words sounded unforgivable when she heard them, but she closed her eyes and pressed on nonetheless. "You know I always leave again."

Erica pushed away from her then. She was still crying, but she wouldn't meet Lilia's eyes anymore. Blue hair falling over her face. She turned and almost seemed to drift as she walked away down the cracked sidewalk, hands deep in her pockets. An empty, narrow-shouldered figure, hair like tropical water and shadows gathering underfoot, slouching and broken on the pre-dawn street. At the corner she turned left and she was gone then, but it was several minutes before Lilia could pick up the suitcase and turn away from the scene of the crime, and she kept looking back. Half expecting that Erica would come running up behind her, half hoping she would.

Lilia stood at the corner with her suitcase waiting for the light to change, and all she could think of was dancing with Erica last night, when she told Erica she was leaving and at first Erica was acting so hopeful and so adorably brave; she gave Lilia her silver chain necklace to wear—"to remember me by," she actually said—and it was a while before it warmed to Lilia's skin. "So you're finally going," Erica said, "just like you said you would." Just like I said I would. I'm sorry. Yes. Tomorrow morning I'll be leaving. The ticket's in my pocket. We are almost out of time. Lilia didn't say, *And you're the first one who ever mattered enough to me to warn in advance that I'm leaving.* "Well, good for you," Erica said. The beginning of the only argument Lilia ever had with her. "I think it's courageous."

Erica's voice trembled a little. She went upstairs to the dance floor and danced ferociously. She was beautiful. Lilia followed her up there and watched her for a while, leaning against a wall, not sure what to do with herself, and then she moved to join Erica in the throng. Thinking as she danced that she could just get a refund on the ticket, that this one time perhaps she could stay, and knowing even in the midst of these thoughts that it was hopeless, that if she didn't leave now she'd only leave later, and Erica danced with her eyes closed, sweat and tears shining on her face. Lilia danced in front of her for a few minutes, but Erica refused to look at her. Later they sat together in the mezzanine of the bar and argued about courage and bus schedules. The second-to-last time Lilia ever saw her.

The last time Lilia saw her she drifted away around the corner, the way newspapers drift when they're caught in slow wind. Every detail of the moment was clear to Lilia later, when she closed her eyes in a departing bus and tortured herself with the scene: Erica disappearing around the corner in the watery pre-dawn light. The striking, final lines of the apartment buildings of this particular neighbourhood, the kind of low ugly buildings that look to stand a fair chance of surviving a nuclear holocaust with their freight of cockroaches intact. The sidewalk shining a little, cement fraught with crushed glass, the neon lights of the restaurant across the street. A police siren in the distance. A decrepit woman passing by on the opposite sidewalk, shuffling unevenly and pushing a cart heaped with cans and old clothing. The quiet stoicism of a man across the street, leaning on the wall of the restaurant. One hand in his pocket, the other on his cane. Watching her, perhaps, from under his fedora.

PART FOUR

36

The day after Lilia's sixteenth birthday, Lilia's father drove through the morning and afternoon. Mirages shimmered on the desert: pools of water appeared on the highway ahead, and the mountains broke from the horizon and floated between the earth and the sky. The heat was unspeakable. She was profoundly happy. Her father drove in silence, every so often blotting sweat from his face with a handkerchief. The dashboard clock marked slow-motion time. They stopped that night in a town the colour of dust where the only restaurants were a McDonald's and a Taco Bell and the Denny's attached to the motel. The waitress who took their breakfast order there in the morning looked hungover, pale and blinking. They'd purchased a new map. Lilia's father studied it carefully.

"We could be in the mountains by afternoon," he said. "Just another few hours of desert."

Lilia had kept the old map, the one that had faded into sepia over nine years of sunlight, and she found herself glancing at it as they drove. The familiarity of those lines. She put on dark glasses and stared out the window. For the first time in several months, she was thinking of her mother. There was always a place in Lilia's mind where her mother existed as a shadow, or perhaps it was the other way around. Not a memory, exactly, more of a ghost. It seemed possible sometimes that Lilia was the one who was haunting her, even from this far away. She was disappearing into sunlight in a second-hand car two days after her sixteenth birthday, and her mother was inconsolable in the distance.

Lilia's mother asleep the night she went away. She didn't hear the sound that woke her daughter up that night, the sharp clear percussion of ice hitting the windowpane from outside. That night Lilia's father put her in the car and wrapped a blanket around her and they drove for a hundred miles through the dark, well over the border; he had their passports ready, and they were waved across. In the northern United States he pulled over and retrieved a silver Thermos from between the seats. He unscrewed the top and poured out a plastic cup of hot chocolate and placed it steaming in her hands. Lilia took it without a word. She hadn't seen him in years, and she was too shy to speak to him yet; she looked down at the gauze bandages and then closed her eyes instead of answering when her father asked if she was okay, and her father touched her face to make her look at him.

"It will be all right," he said. "I promise." She stared up at him and sipped the chocolate and nodded. Her memories of that night held no trace of regret.

But nine years later she closed her eyes in a car in the desert, and despite the happiness of the moment she was shot through with doubt. It was beginning to dawn on her that she had travelled so long, so perfectly, that it was difficult to conceive of another kind of life. It was difficult to imagine stopping, but stopping was imminent. In a few days they were going back to Stillspell, to Clara's house in the desert, Clara's creaky staircases and blue rooms and morning coffee.

"Aren't you looking forward to staying there?" her father asked. "Not travelling anymore?"

"I'm not sure I know how to stay," Lilia said.

37

"Did she ever give you an explanation?" Michaela asked. She had hair like cartoon lightning, hard and spiky, she ran her hands through it and it stood on end. She had dyed her hair that afternoon. Black hair, black bustier, black vinyl miniskirt. Everything about her reminded Eli of midnight. He sat at the small wooden table behind her, watching her reflection, overwhelmed by her presence, her ferocious green eyes, trying to think of something to say. The palms of his hands were pressed to the tabletop, and he could feel the vibration of the music upstairs.

"How late did you sleep?" he asked instead of answering her. He had left her asleep on the carpet the previous morning, walking back to the hotel past the amused stares of desk clerks, up to the dim early-morning grey of the room, where he'd fallen asleep instantly on top of the covers. In the early afternoon he sat for a long time in a café not far from Club Electrolite, composing a rambling letter to Zed. He'd gone so far as to buy stamps, but it wasn't clear to him whether he would mail it. The envelope was folded in half in his jacket pocket, along with the page from the Gideon Bible that Lilia had written on as a child, and from time to time— he never took his jacket off anymore, even indoors—he would reach into his pocket and run his fingers over the envelope just to be sure it was still there.

"I don't know," she said, "mid-afternoon. Then I got up and dyed my hair."

"It looks nice," he said.

"Thank you."

"Have you eaten?"

"No."

"Are you hungry?"

"Not really." She was drawing a dark pencil outline around the edges of her lipstick. "Do you think anyone would miss me if I didn't go out?"

"No one would miss you," he said. "You're like a part of the night."

Anyone else would have taken that badly, but she was smiling as she set her lip-liner pencil down on the countertop. They were quiet for a while, Eli looking down at the ruined surface of the table. Someone had stubbed out a great many cigarettes on the wood, over a long period of time. The surface was scarred with dark craters and lines.

"How long have you been here?" Michaela asked.

He looked up. She leaned back in her chair, studied herself in the mirror for a second, and began searching for a slightly darker shade of lipstick. Her pale hand hovered over the chaos of tubes and jars on the countertop.

"Two weeks," he said. "I'm about to max out my last credit card." The weight of the fourteen days in this city descended like a curtain over everything, and he couldn't see her for a moment.

She made a sound that could have been a laugh. She'd found the lipstick she'd been searching for and she was applying it slowly, her lips turning to a shade midway between black and blood-red.

"My fellow sailor," she said. "Did she ever give you an explanation?"

"I don't want to talk about this."

She glanced at him in the mirror. "Two acquaintances," she said, "two friends, two fellow sailors marooned together on a hostile ice floe, speaking the wrong language, talking about an accident that occurred six or seven years ago in another country." She was putting gel in her hair, making it harder and spikier. "What harm would it do?"

He sighed.

"Why not tell me? She betrayed you."

"She didn't—"

"She *left*."

He stared down at the tabletop.

"When you find her," she said, "when you finally find her, do you really think she'll come home with you, after all this?"

"No," he said. "I don't. I just want to make sure she's all right."

A long time passed in silence, while she sprayed something in her hair and then brushed silver powder over her eyelids.

"Michaela," he said finally, "I would do a great deal for you. But I can't tell you what you want to know."

"You know," she said, "I was thinking earlier today, while I was dyeing my hair, I was thinking my father and you have a lot in common. You were both left by Lilia."

"You were left by Lilia too."

She sat still for a moment, looking at her reflection, and then rose and moved past him to the clothing rack. There was a new-looking plastic bag hanging from one of the cheap wire hangers; she tore it open and pulled out a pair of black feathery wings. They were the sort of thing a child might wear on Halloween night, fluffy and not very large. She slipped the elastic loops over her bony shoulders and spent a few minutes trying to make them even in the mirror.

"Jacques bought them for me," she said. "So I'll be like the sign."

He watched her. She smiled at herself and did one slow turn in the mirror, admiring the wings from every angle. She was beautiful to him. He had an image of Michaela as a little girl, dressing up for Halloween in a pair of angel wings in the years before her parents left her, and he closed his eyes.

"If I told you . . ." he began, "if I *did* tell you, would you promise . . ." and instantly regretted saying even this much, but it was already too late; she was already moving around the table to kneel in front of his chair, there were already tears in her eyes, she was already holding his hands in her own, and Lilia, far away in a previous life, was already careening toward the accident in the backseat of her father's car.

38

In a bar on the outskirts of Ellington, New Mexico, a few miles from the town of Stillspell, Christopher was sitting alone with a whiskey and planning his departure from the United States. It was evening, the day after Lilia's sixteenth birthday, and Lilia was moving ever farther away. He was aware that she was somewhere to the north, and frightened by his awareness. He didn't see Clara come in. She slipped onto the barstool beside him and ordered a Coke without looking at him.

"I don't know anything," she said, "first of all."

"Right." He struggled to flatten his voice and make his accent longer and more Southern, more American.

"But let's say I knew someone," she said. "Let's say I knew someone who knew someone."

He nodded.

"I mean, suppose I knew someone who'd been, for a very long time, perhaps years, inviting a fugitive . . ." She glanced around theatrically and lowered her voice. "What if she'd been inviting a fugitive into her home for a long time? A criminal. Would she be implicated?"

"Not if she were ignorant of his crimes."

"What if she weren't?"

"Well," he said, "then I suppose it's something else."

"What if she'd seen this man . . . what if she'd seen him on television, with his little girl, before she even *met* him, what if she knew exactly who he was when she saw him in person for the first time, but never let on and never told anyone?"

"For Christ's sake, Clara, stop speaking in the third person. I'm not asking you to turn him in."

"But I thought you were," she said, and turned white when she realized what she'd said.

"Listen," he said, "I approached you for a reason, and it wasn't to get to him. I don't want you to ever go to the police, do you understand?"

"I wasn't planning on it," she replied indistinctly.

"No, you're not planning on it, but you might get scared, and the thought might cross your mind. You might get into a fight with him, you might wake up one day and decide you're sick of wondering why he did it. I can see that you're pregnant, and you might be panicking because you're going to have his child and you're not convinced that he won't take that child away too, you might do something unplanned and regrettable and tell someone before you realize what you're doing, and I'm asking you not to."

"Why would you ask that?"

"It's never black and white," he said. "You know it was an abduction. But what if he saved his child?"

"I'm afraid I don't quite—"

"No," he said, "you *do* follow. Stay with me here. Look, it isn't the best parent who gains custody. It's just the one with the best lawyer."

She was silent.

"Even setting the question of lawyers aside for a moment," Christopher said, "the mother almost always gets custody. It's just the way it is. Imagine that his ex-wife wouldn't let him see their daughter, imagine that she'd obtained a restraining order for absolutely no good reason whatsoever, so that the man was barred from approaching his daughter by legal means. And then, after all this, imagine that the child was in danger and had been hurt once, badly. Imagine if he was alerted to this, and the only action he could think of was to take her away in the middle of the night? Once he'd done that, there was no undoing that moment. It never was possible to stop taking her away, once he started. He's still taking her away, because he's still taking care of her."

Clara was very still, looking at her glass.

"Listen," he said, "I've been working on this case for years now. I interviewed her brother a few months ago, finally, and he—"

"What took you so long?" she asked indistinctly.

"It's a long story. A contract expired. Clara, listen, I know what happened to her. I know why she has scars on her arms. It's still an abduction, it's still against the law, but imagine that he saved her life. Wouldn't that mitigate everything else? Absolutely everything?" He was silent for a moment, toying with his hat on the bar. "Her father took her away because he felt he had to, and if you care for either of them, never go to the police. That's all I wanted to say to you."

There were tears on her face. "Thank you," she said.

He left her there and went back to his car in the half-empty parking lot. He drove back past the Stillspell Motel, past the Morning Star Diner with all its windows alight. The highway was almost empty. He drove well above the speed limit, covering ground. In a car somewhere far ahead, Lilia was singing along to the radio with her father. They had left New Mexico. They would stop at a motel soon. It was getting late. But Christopher, behind them, drove through the night.

"Are you still awake?" Lilia whispered. It was the middle of October, and a crescent moon was rising outside the bedroom window of the apartment in Brooklyn. She was sitting cross-legged on the bed, and Eli was lying on his back beside her in the darkness. She had been speaking softly for nearly a half-hour, telling a long story about cars and motel rooms and driving away, and he was listening in perfect silence.

"Of course I'm awake. It was your sixteenth birthday. Clara brought home a cake."

"Right," she said. "We ate cake up on the rooftop, and then the next day we left. It was just a short trip we were taking, gone for a few days and then back home to Stillspell, but the day after we left there was an accident."

"A car accident? Were you hurt?"

"You have to promise never to tell anyone."

"Sure," he said.

"No, promise you won't tell anyone this part, no matter what, even a long time from now, even if you're angry with me."

"Why would I be angry with you?" In sixteen days she would leave him and travel away again, but only one of them knew that.

"Just promise you won't tell anyone, no matter what."

"Okay," he said, "I promise. No matter what."

On a narrow highway in the mountains, old and in considerable disrepair, two cars moved quickly under a brilliant sky. The car in front was a small grey Toyota, purchased specifically because it was absolutely forgettable. The car travelling behind was a sky-blue Chrysler Valiant with Quebec licence plates, and it had been directly behind the Toyota for nearly an hour. There was a newer highway nearby—wider, safer, with a less calamitous drop-off on the right shoulder—but the first car had pulled onto the old highway an hour ago, and the second car was in pursuit. Lilia's father swerved around potholes, a fallen branch, hands clenched on the steering wheel. Sometime earlier he had turned off the radio. Now he drove ten miles above the speed limit in charged speechlessness, and ten miles above the speed limit wasn't fast enough.

"I don't know what to do," he said finally, quietly. For him, this was an extraordinary admission. He pulled over sharply to the side of the highway and cut the engine. The blue Valiant slowed as it moved past them and pulled over on the shoulder of the road ahead. In that moment before the driver's-side door opened, the stillness was nearly absolute.

The man who emerged from the car had an almost spindly look about him. He was tall and slump-shouldered, in a rumpled brown blazer and faded blue jeans. He wore a brown fedora, which he removed as he approached. He carried it in both hands in front of him, like a present. Lilia's father rolled down his window, and the only sounds were the man's footsteps approaching on the pavement, and wind in the pine trees by the sides of the road. Her father's other hand was on the key.

The man rested his forearm on the roof of the car, looking in. He didn't look like an FBI agent.

"I'm sorry to disturb you," he said. He spoke with the softest traces of Lilia's mother's accent. "It's just that I've been travelling alongside you for a while. For quite some time." He was looking directly at Lilia, frozen in the passenger seat. "I'm going home tomorrow, and I won't be coming back to this country again. I just wanted to tell you that you don't need to travel anymore."

"I don't know what you're talking about," Lilia's father said.

"Look, I understand why you did it," the detective said. "I have a daughter in Montreal, and I wish I'd done the same sometimes." A car was approaching. It passed in a blur of red and the detective was quiet for a moment, watching it recede. "I spoke to Simon last year, and I know why you did what you did. I know what happened that night. I just wanted to say goodbye, to wish you the best, I just wanted to tell you—"

"I don't understand what you're talking about. You've mistaken me for someone else."

"You ever heard the story of Icarus?" the detective asked. "I've been reading it recently. If you'll forgive me speaking in such flowery terms, John, this is what it comes down to: I don't mind not being the hero of the story, I don't mind being the shepherd watching you fly out over the sea with your child, but I don't want to be the Minotaur." He sighed. He was looking at Lilia now. "I don't know how else to put it," he said. "I just don't want to chase you anymore. I'm going to say I couldn't find you, and that'll be it. That'll be it. I don't think anyone else is looking for you anymore."

Lilia's father was staring straight ahead through the windshield, not speaking, but Lilia saw a muscle working frantically in his jaw. She had never before heard anyone use her father's real name.

"Good luck," said Christopher. "Lilia." He stared at her for a moment longer and smiled. "A pleasure to see you, as always. Your brother sends his regards. Happy birthday, my love." He straightened, and put on his hat. Lilia sat still beside her father, watching Christopher recede. The detective started his car and drove away, disappeared around a bend in the highway ahead and was lost behind the pine trees, and only then did her father turn the key in the ignition.

It took her a few minutes to realize that he was still driving too fast.

"You don't know your mother," he said when she glanced at him. His voice was hoarse and he'd gone pale. There was sweat on his forehead.

"He said he wasn't going to chase us anymore." She felt sick.

"It's exactly the kind of thing she'd tell him to say. You don't know your mother, it's exactly the kind of thing she'd . . ." The blue car had come into sight up ahead. "She will never stop chasing you," her father said. "She will never give you up." The detective was driving slowly now, like a sightseer. He was driving one-handed, resting his other arm on the edge of the open window. He craned his neck briefly to look up; Lilia followed his gaze and saw the mountains, the sheer rock just visible above the trees to the left. "Lilia," her father said, abruptly calm, "get in the backseat behind me, and put on your seat belt."

The highway turned and twisted through dark pine forest. In the seat behind him Lilia pressed her face to the glass to look up at the sky. She wanted to be anywhere else in the world. There were hawks circling in the high blue air. The Valiant was very close now, and she forced herself to look at it. She saw the detective glance up into his rear-view mirror. He raised his hand to wave, uncomprehending.

"Lilia," said her father, "cover your eyes."

She didn't cover her eyes. Her father was pulling alongside the detective's car; he glanced back and forth between the detective's car and the highway ahead, and then slowly, with methodical precision, he began to turn the wheel to the right. The grind and screech of metal on metal was unbearable, but she couldn't look away, and both cars were moving toward the edge of the road. Lilia's father was looking out the passenger-side window, judging the distance and the degree of force required, gradually easing the other car off the road. There was a very short period when it seemed possible that the detective might still manage to stay on the highway, might still swerve to safety at the very last possible instant and speed ahead and make it after all, but her father gave the wheel one last, barely perceptible turn, so that Christopher's car left the highway altogether and began a sideways, almost slow-motion slide off the edge of the embankment, down the hill, flipping slowly over onto its side and then upside down and then out of sight as she turned to watch out the back window, and she heard the nerve-shattering impact of metal around the trunk of a tree.

It wasn't the accident itself that broke her, but the way he surrendered to it. It seemed, no matter how she tried to reconfigure the moment in her memory, that the detective was ready for the accident. There was a fleeting moment when he met Lilia's eyes, just at the end: he smiled and allowed his car to slide over the edge. He made no discernible effort to stay on the road.

41

Michaela rose from the floor of the dressing room and left the room without speaking, picking her jacket up off the floor as she went, pulling it on over her lopsided wings. Eli followed her up the stairs, lost her in the crowds on the dance floor, and found her again on the frozen sidewalk outside, shivering and speaking into her cell phone. "I don't care," she said, "meet me there anyway." She put the cell phone in her jacket pocket and looked at him as if they'd never met.

"Michaela?"

"Eli," she said.

"Who were you talking to?"

She looked at him without answering. There was a blankness about her. He wasn't sure if she'd heard him.

"I told you the story," he said. "Now you have to tell me where she is."

"I don't know. She was here the night you came." She began walking away from him, unsteady on the ice. He reached out to steady her, and they walked together arm in arm. "She *was* in the dressing room that night, before I brought you down there. I guess I should've brought you down sooner, before she had a chance to leave." She stopped, pulled her arm away from his, fumbled in her jacket pocket. "She said she'd wait for me in the dressing room till I came back," she muttered. "Fucking liar." She extracted a pack of cigarettes and a lighter from her jacket.

"People fail you," he said impatiently. "It's a chance you take. Where's Lilia?"

"I don't know," she said. "She left. She was supposed to be

in my dressing room when you . . . *fuck*," she said. The lighter was clicking uselessly. "You have a light?"

There were two matchbooks in his pocket. He didn't smoke but had at some point acquired the habit of compulsively collecting promotional matchbooks from restaurants.

"You want Les Deux Gamins matches or Café Universel matches?"

She gave him a blankly vicious look, like a wild creature deprived of food. He gave her both matchbooks.

"Your pronunciation's terrible," she said when the cigarette was safely ignited. They'd made slow, wavering progress to a street corner. The light changed to red just as they reached the edge of the sidewalk. She was shivering. He took her arm again and she leaned into him silently.

"I'm sorry, Michaela. It's an awful story." The cold was agonizing. He'd never imagined this quality of wind. It was possible to imagine his blood freezing under his skin, and there was ice in his eyelashes. It was eleven P.M. on a Sunday, and Rue Sainte-Catherine was all but deserted. Neon signs flickered from behind the barred windows of clubs. *Girls Girls Girls. Danseuses Nues.*

"I need to find Lilia," he said.

She laughed. "You'd be amazed at how many people have said that in her lifetime. I don't know where she is."

"You have to know, you promised to tell me. Is she still in the city?"

She didn't answer. They'd crossed the street and were heading slowly downhill, past the Musique Plus building, past electronics stores and closed cafés. They were passing into a surreal public space that he'd walked past many times without venturing into, a sweeping expanse of concrete and terraced steps. It was lit by regularly spaced black lampposts, each holding five round orbs of blue light. In the midst of all this was a frozen rectangular pool.

Michaela seemed exhausted. She was leaning on his arm, breathing heavily. She broke away from him to climb the steps, sat down haltingly about halfway to the top. She stayed there in an apparent daze, smoking, while he shivered up and down and tried to figure out what to do. Her teeth were chattering. After a couple of minutes he sat beside her, wrapped his arms around his body, and tried to convince himself that he would someday regain feeling in his toes.

"Well, look," he said, "when did you see her last?"

She opened her box of cigarettes, extracted one, and lit it expertly with the remains of its predecessor. She tossed the old one away, toward the street. He watched it smoulder for an instant on the ice. She didn't seem likely to answer him, so he tried another tack.

"What's this place called?"

"Place-des-Arts. It's nicer in summer." She removed the cigarette from her mouth, studied it while she exhaled.

"I think," said Eli, "that we should probably keep moving. It can't be more than twenty degrees out."

She glanced at him briefly. "I don't know Fahrenheit."

"It's no warmer in Celsius. The point is that we're going to die out here. We should go," he said, but Michaela was weeping. She swept tears away from her face with one shaking hand and held the cigarette loosely with the other. Ashes drifted to the snow.

"I always thought I wanted to know what happened," she said.

"Hey," he said helplessly, "it'll be all right. We just have to keep walking. We'll go somewhere, my sailor, we'll go to the café, I'll buy you tea . . ."

She was pulling herself up by a metal railing, shaking her head.

"I don't want *tea*," she said.

He held her shoulder to steady her, and her silver jacket

was shining in the blue lights of the plaza. He looked away from her, toward the long expanse of Rue Sainte-Catherine. A nightmare of locked doors and closed restaurants and buzzing neon signs, panhandlers begging to be rescued from the cold, wrong city, and he wished to be absolutely anywhere else. He wished he had never walked into the Café Matisse in Brooklyn, or at least that he'd waited for his own table instead of sitting down with Lilia. He wished he had been paying attention on the morning she'd left and stopped her on her way out the door. He wished, if those previous wishes had failed, that at least he hadn't followed her here. An eternal half-life in Brooklyn, he thought, an eternal half-life of posers and unfinished manuscripts and fake artists and failed scholarship and guilt-inducing phone calls from his mother and letters from his unmatchable and unsurpassable brother would have been better than an hour of this.

"I don't understand how you can live in a place this cold," he said.

"I can't. I'll be leaving soon." She started up the steps, and he stepped close to hold her arm again. They were passing slowly over the concrete plaza away from Rue Sainte-Catherine, stepping carefully on ice, Rue Ontario deserted on the other side. "Do you know what Lilia said about this city?"

The name still made his heart constrict in his chest.

"What did she say about it?"

"She said she'd travelled one city too far. She said she wished she'd never left New York."

And there in the concrete plaza, the weight of centuries and continents lifted away from him into the night. He was suddenly, absurdly, fantastically light. She wished she'd never left him. This could all be undone. He could have leapt into the air just then and never landed, but he stayed on the ground and seized her shoulders instead.

"Please tell me where she is."

"You'll go back to Brooklyn with her," she said, "and I'll still be here."

"You just said you were leaving."

"She only stayed with me because she wanted me to tell her what happened that night, why she had those scars on her arms. I only stayed with her because I wanted her to tell me about an accident, and now that you've told me, I wish I didn't know." There was an uneven quality to her voice, and her eyes were too bright. "Did you notice them?"

"Notice what?"

"The *scars*," she said.

"Of course I did."

"Her mother threw her through a window." She fumbled in her pockets again; she lit another cigarette and smiled terribly. "That's the part of the story she doesn't know, the part she doesn't remember. Partial amnesia is the most remarkable thing."

"Jesus Christ," he said.

"Fortunately," said Michaela, "it'd snowed heavily the night before. Cushioned the fall, I'd imagine. Probably saved her life."

"I don't want to know any of this. All I want to know is where she is."

"No," she said, "you need to know the story, so you can tell it to her when you see her next. I'm not sure if I'm going to see her again. So listen to me, this will just take a second: her mother threw her through a window. She was seven years old. She lay in the snow until her brother came out to get her."

"Her brother?"

"Simon. He was nine or ten at the time. Simon said the mother was hysterical, weeping and carrying on. She told Simon much later that she never knew what it was about

Lilia that made her want to annihilate her so desperately, but there it is: she throws her seven-year-old daughter through a window at night and leaves her outside in the snow. Remember, we're talking about Quebec in the wintertime. It was probably as cold that night as it is now."

He was silent, watching her.

"Simon went outside to get her. Lilia had landed in a deep snowdrift outside the window. Nothing was broken, but she had cuts all over her arms from the glass. He got her back into the house and put towels around her arms to stop the bleeding, and then he called Lilia's father, his ex-stepfather. He told his sister's father to come get her. Do you understand? Her own brother arranged her abduction," she said.

It took him a moment to recover his voice. "Lilia doesn't remember this?"

"None of it. She doesn't know what happened. There was a first-aid kit somewhere in the house. Simon bandaged his sister's arms as best he could, got her upstairs and put her to bed and lay down to wait in the room next door. He left the front door unlocked. Lilia's father came late that night and saw the broken glass in the snow, just like Simon told him. When Lilia came downstairs, her father took her away. Amazing, isn't it? That's the moment when Lilia's memories begin. Her father throws broken glass at her bedroom window, and she hears the sound and sits up in bed."

"Michaela, you have to tell me where she is."

"Fairly close by, I imagine. She rents a room not far from here." She held her cigarette up in the air. "My last cigarette," she announced. "I'm quitting tonight."

"Good. You smoke too much."

"I'm going into the metro," Michaela said. She stepped backward. "Which way are you going?"

"I don't know yet, Michaela. You have to tell me where to go."

"Why should I?" She was more interested in the cigarette. She inhaled deeply, looked at it for a second, and then dropped it half finished into the snow.

"I am so tired," Eli said. "It's so cold out here. I want to go home."

She took a few more steps backward, away from him. He watched the movements of her sleek boots on the precarious ice. The toes were scuffed. "She's been renting a room on Rue de la Visitation," she said finally. "Corner of Rue Ontario, in Centre-Sud. You just follow Ontario that way, ten or so blocks. It's the brown building on the southwest corner, across from a restaurant that used to be a gas station. Her building sort of sags outward toward the street. There're always transvestite hookers in front of it." She gestured in a northeasterly direction. "Say goodbye to her for me?"

"I will." He was moving away from her, waving, already somewhere else. "Thank you," he said. "I'll call you tomorrow."

She turned away without answering. He watched her recede for a moment and then began walking as fast as he could over the ice. East on Ontario toward Rue de la Visitation, and even this coldest of cities seemed suddenly exquisite to him. The blank cement architecture was refreshingly clean-lined. The wide empty streets were calm instead of lifeless. The cold was almost bracing. The exhaustion that had settled over him in the weeks since she'd gone was beginning to lift, slowly, in increments too small to be individually observed, the way mist rises from a river in the morning. *She wished she'd never left New York.*

He didn't get very close to Rue de la Visitation. Michaela's last few words were pulling at him—*Say goodbye to her for me?*—and near the corner of Saint-Laurent, he understood. Eli stopped as if shot in the amber streetlight and turned back the way he had come. Walking quickly at first, but then he broke into a run, back toward the parking lot, gasping in the ice-locked air. His teeth hurt with each footstep on the frozen pavement, the cold burning his face. He ran back to Place-des-Arts in the staggering cold, he threw himself down the stairs of the Métro Place-des-Arts station and ran past the ticket booth, vaulting over a turnstile and running faster, down to the level of fast underground trains, faster still, but the girl at the far end of the westbound platform had been standing there for several minutes by the time he saw her, and the trains were running slightly ahead of schedule that night. It was warm down here. She had taken off her silver jacket and folded it neatly on a nearby bench. The Halloween wings were still on her back, although now they were lopsided, and an empty red cigarette box was crushed in one hand.

Although the subway lines of all cities differ in details, the sequence of events is more or less the same: first a slight wind down the length of the tunnel, a few seconds before even the sound of the train. Then (depending on the city, the design of the subway system, the specifics of the individual station) there are a few seconds or even a full minute of approaching light, twin beams through the darkness, and by now the approaching thunder of sound. By the time Eli reached the platform, pursued by a police officer who'd watched him jump the turnstile at the ticket booth, he could already see the lights. Approaching at a merciless speed into the station, closer and closer to the waiting girl. There were people on the platform, some looking at him now as he ran— he thought he heard someone say his name—but he was aware of no one but Michaela in that moment.

It's possible that she didn't hear him screaming her name as he ran full speed down the platform toward her. She was utterly intent on what she was about to do just then, poised on the edge with one foot slightly forward, like a tightrope walker about to step out onto the rope. She was looking at the approaching lights.

Eli was screaming in formless sounds now—although the pursuing official hadn't noticed the girl and kept calling out for him to stop in perfectly comprehensible French—but screaming halts nothing.

In the instant before the train would have passed her, the girl stepped forward into the onslaught of air.

Sometimes at night Simon still thinks of his sister's departure, of watching from the landing window as Lilia's father carried her away across the lawn, the way she clung so tightly to her father's neck—the bandages Simon had put on her arms a few hours earlier stark white in the moonlight—until they disappeared into the forest. There's a number that he dials sometimes from memory, on nights when he can't sleep. He pressed *69 once, when he was very young, and wrote the number down on his hand. No one ever picks up, but he's soothed by the crackle of static over the line, and there's a pleasing sense of bridging tremendous distance. The ringing sounds unfathomably far away.

There is a pay phone by a truck stop near the town of Leonard, Arizona. Sometimes at night it starts to ring.

Eli's bed was the hull of a fishing boat. An antique figurehead had been mounted on the bow. In daylight she took the form of a woman rising out of foam, her eyes burning a path toward the North Star and morning. Her hair had been painted the colour of fire, her eyes a terrible and final blue. In her arms she held a fish: an hour by subway from the nearest ocean, it opened its gasping mouth to the sky.

Her eyes guarded the door to his bedroom, which had been painted like the entrance to a pirate's cave, and he was grateful for her presence. In the first days after the hospital, his blood heavy with memory and sedatives, he felt too sick to be alone in the room. Nothing in the room, he found, was quite real. This had been the case since mid-childhood, but it was more problematic these days than it had been. The walls were blue, and streaked with lighter and darker shades that made them look watery in certain lights. This effect had been noticed by his brother when they were nine and eleven, and they'd spent a few weeks painting desert islands and fish. Their mother, who had a great love of consistency, had installed the figurehead bed the following year. The room was a dreamish seascape, more amateurish in some places than in others because Zed, besides being two years older, was a better painter than Eli. In bad moments Eli thought he might be drowning, but he didn't want to say anything or request a move to another bedroom. He felt bad about all the trouble everyone had already gone to.

It hadn't been easy to retrieve him from Montreal. The hospital had lost his wallet. This was hardly unprecedented, but in this particular case it was unusually disastrous, because with the wallet missing somewhere in the understaffed chaos of the emergency room and the patient in no mood to illuminate anyone, no one knew the patient's name. The police liked to come by occasionally, particularly in the first few days, and ask leading questions from the chair next to the bed, alternating hopefully between English and French. The patient would reply in neither language and stared blankly or tearfully out the window instead.

In those days Eli existed in a state of profound distraction. He was deeply preoccupied with watching the same two nightmares playing over and over and over again on an agonizingly continuous loop. The first was a speeded-up version of Lilia leaving his apartment in Brooklyn. This had happened some time before he had arrived at the hospital, but the details remained brilliant: she stands before the sofa running her fingers through her still damp hair, she kisses him on the head for the third time that morning, she announces that she's going for the paper, the door closes and he hears her footsteps going down the stairs. The other involved a train, a girl holding a crushed red cigarette box, and the brownish interior of the Métro Place-des-Arts station in downtown Montreal. He closed his eyes in the hospital and saw the way the tightrope walker stepped out into the empty air, sans tightrope, the way the small dark figure was suspended for an instant in front of the blue train until she fell and was lost in the thudding conspiracy of machinery and rails and heavy dark wheels, now slick. He fell down by the platform edge and this was where he was plucked from, later. He'd thought he heard Lilia's voice. Later he woke in a pale blank room, unspeaking, and this was where he remained for weeks after the fact, lost in distraction while a succession of professionals passed through his hospital room. He was aware of them in flashes: the police officer who changed into a nurse, then a doctor, then a nice lady with a lump of clay for him to express himself with, then a chair. He couldn't hear their questions over the din of the train, but the procession continued on looped replay (nurse, doctor, doctor, chair) until the morning when Zed walked into the room.

Eli wasn't looking at the door. The fragile wintery light through the window had held his attention for hours. But (here, a sudden miracle) all at once Zed's voice was in this room, in this city, and Eli turned his face toward it. He hadn't seen his brother in a year and a half.

Zed was speaking rapidly in French to one nurse among several, his eyes never leaving Eli's face and his voice brimming with impatience. Eli heard his own name repeated twice. Zed kept up a rapid monologue as he corralled a small crowd of concerned medical professionals toward the exit. With the phantoms safely exiled to the hallway, he closed the door, held it shut for a second lest anyone get any clever ideas, turned back to Eli, and finally smiled. He approached the bed, turned the chair around, and sat sideways on it.

"Hello," Eli said. This was, at least, the intent. After twenty-seven days without talking, it came out as a whispery croak. He swallowed.

"Eli. Good morning. Why wouldn't you tell them your name?"

"I didn't feel like talking," Eli said, slightly more audibly.

Zed laughed quietly and went to the window. The low skyline was blurred by falling snow.

"I didn't know you spoke French," Eli said.

"I picked it up over the years."

"I tried to jump after her."

"I know. They told me," his brother said.

"I'm always too late, Zed. I'm always just a beat too late."

"Everyone's too late sometimes."

"Have you ever seen what a train does to a girl?"

Zed was silent for a moment, looking out the window.

"This place is dire," he said finally. "I'm taking you home."

What followed was a complicated, unbearable sequence, difficult to remember in detail later on. A red vinyl chair at an airport in Dorval, just outside the city of Montreal. A check-in counter on which he leaned heavily and stared at the floor. Wheelchairs had been offered. He insisted on walking through the airport but couldn't remember what direction he was meant to be walking in for more than a minute. Zed, laden with luggage and worry, was forever seizing him by the elbow and realigning him. Eli had an odd way of walking: shuffling, tripful, stumbling over shadows on the smooth glossy floor.

A brief flight over a border in wintertime. The grey wing of a plane outside the window. The world glimpsed in barely remembered flashes of snow and air and the corners of buildings (memories of a dream he'd had once: snow, wartime, the vague impression of heroism, hiding in a ditch in the cold). The streets of Manhattan through the windows of a taxicab. ("At least it's *alive* here," he said to his brother, before he closed his eyes again. It was the first thing he'd said in four hours, and did nothing to reassure Zed.) Their mother reduced to a kind of concerned impression, insubstantial and far-off, like a sketch of a mother drawn on transparent architect's vellum. A door opening into the blue room where he'd slept as a child, assurances that he could rest here as long as he needed to and that everything was going to be all right, pyjamas, the sound of worried voices out in the hallway afterward. He closed his eyes and went to sleep immediately.

In the first few days he didn't move very much. He lay still on the bed watching light move across the ceiling. Later on the days assumed a particular rhythm: cadences of winter light in the clear afternoons, the white-and-black expanse of Central Park out the window of his mother's apartment, white snow and silvery trees and dark paths winding between them—he could lose himself in this vision for hours on end. There were entire afternoons when life distilled into precisely this: a blue room on the Upper West Side and snow outside the window, his mother's favourite Bach or Vivaldi playing quietly somewhere in another room and his mother humming tunelessly along with it, and people passing small and dark in the icy world below.

"The question," Zed remarked, "is what you're going to do now."

Zed wasn't staying much longer. He was going back to Africa for a few weeks, and after that he was making plans to go to Europe. He wanted, he said, to sit where the oracle had sat at Delphi. He wanted Eli to come with him. They had half-hearted arguments on whether there was still an oracle there; Eli thought there might be. Zed tended toward the school of thought that all of us are oracles, but was inclined to believe that this particular one no longer walked the earth.

"I want to travel."

"I meant after Greece. After our trip. Are you going back to Brooklyn?"

"To Brooklyn? No, I don't think so."

"Why not?"

"Because nothing I did there *meant* anything," Eli said. "Because I was ice-skating in that life as much as she was. I do have friends there, but I think I'd rather be . . ." He hesitated, looking at a solitary man walking into the park, his coat dark against the snowy path, and he pressed his fingertips against the glass. "I haven't been outside in a while," he said. "I'd like to immerse myself in all that."

"In all what?"

"That was her problem," Eli said. "She couldn't immerse herself. It isn't enough to observe the world and take pictures of it." He was quiet for a second and then said, "It isn't enough to just go ice-skating. Lilia's metaphor, not mine—she was talking about how she lived. About how you can skate over the surface of the world for your entire life, visiting, leaving, without ever really falling through. But you can't do that, it isn't good enough. You have to be able to fall through. You have to be able to sink, to immerse yourself. You can't just skate over the surface and visit and leave."

"Some people only know how to skate."

"How did you find me in Montreal?"

"There was an unmailed letter to me in your jacket pocket."

"Do you still have it?"

It was in Zed's pocket. He passed it over to Eli without a word. It was longer than Eli remembered, four or five pages wadded tightly together. The writing was wild and allowed for no margins, words crashing up against the edges of the page:

I wanted to be her North Star. I wanted to be her map. I was alone before I met her. I wanted to disappear with her, and fold her into my life. I wanted to be her compass. I wanted to be her last speaker, her interpreter, her language. I wanted to be her translator, Zed, but none of the languages we knew were the same.

"I don't even recognize the handwriting," Eli said.

"Any idea where she went?"

"No idea. She could be anywhere by now. I actually thought I heard her voice on the train platform in Montreal, but I think I was hallucinating." He was looking at the letter. "This is like a dispatch from a foreign country," he said. He refolded it carefully and gave it back to Zed. "I mean, technically it *is* a dispatch from a foreign country, it's just, I don't recognize . . ."

"The handwriting? The sentiment?"

"Both, actually. Neither."

"You don't still wish you could be with her?"

"I think I'd rather be alone," he said.

On her last morning in Montreal Lilia woke early, and lay still for a while under the blankets. She slept fully clothed in those days and wore two pairs of socks to bed, but winter seeped through the windows of her rented room. She rose and showered quickly, shivering, and put on her waitressing uniform. At the Bistro de Porto down the street she fell into the trance of work, cleaning and serving, and in the late afternoon she went back to her room and changed out of the uniform. Out on the street again she wandered for some hours, but it was too cold to take photographs. She didn't want to take her hands out of her pockets. She walked past Club Electrolite in the early evening, half hoping to catch a glimpse of Michaela again, but there was no one out front. She spent some time in her favourite bookstore, reading a history of New York City in French, and then started home in the gathering night. The cold in Montreal was like nothing she'd experienced. She was wearing three sweaters under her jacket, but none of them were thick enough, and her clenched hands felt like ice in her gloves. She stopped for a while in an all-night coffee shop in Centre-Sud to read the paper, trying to avoid the loneliness of her rented room, and she was just stepping out into the darkness again when her cell phone rang. Only Michaela and her employer knew the number.

"I want you to meet me somewhere," Michaela said.

"Why?"

"Meet me on the westbound platform at Métro Place-des-Arts. I'll tell you what you want to know."

"You've said that before. I don't believe you."

"I don't care," Michaela said. "Meet me there anyway."

Two hours later Lilia was in a taxi to the airport, staring blankly at the passing night. She flew from Montreal to Rome at three in the morning, Rome chosen because it was the flight leaving soonest when she arrived at the airport that night and she knew how to speak the language. She withdrew the contents of her bank account from an airport ATM and paid for the ticket in cash. She looked out the airplane window into darkness through all of the long transatlantic night, weeping intermittently, and in the early-morning light she disembarked from a taxi in the Piazza di Popolo. Later she stood on a bridge over the Tiber River and let the three lists fall from her hands: a list of names, ten pages, beginning and ending with *Lilia;* a list of places, nine pages, beginning and ending with the province of Quebec; a shorter list of words, of phrases, all Eli's. She had to leave quickly then because a policeman was approaching meaningfully from the Trastevere side of the bridge, apparently having observed her dropping pieces of paper into the Tiber, so she didn't get to watch the pieces of her old life float away the way she had wanted to.

Lilia walked quickly down the boulevard that ran alongside the river, hands in her pockets in the morning light, and the city foremost in her mind at that moment wasn't Montreal or New York or even Chicago, but San Diego. A place far back toward the genesis of everything, a version of herself so distant that the memory itself was third-person: Lilia, young and unstable and awakened frequently by nightmares about a car accident in the mountains, prone to weeping in moments of frenzy or disarray. Lilia, sixteen years old and unaware of her own story, still in shock from an accident a month or two before, fervent and always running out of time, arriving in San Diego alone after dark. Her father and Clara had said goodbye in New Mexico and given her money, made her promise to call and write and come back to visit before too much time had passed. San Diego was the first city she'd ever travelled to by herself, they were terrified and knew they couldn't stop her, and she was shocked by the exhilaration of solo travel. She pressed her forehead against the bus window and watched the landscape passing by, anguished and exultant and perfectly free. In those days she was tightly wound and always ready to cry, and life seemed fraught with an almost unbearable intensity. In the bus on the way to San Diego she saw a dead cat by the side of the highway, recent roadkill, and she burst into hysterical tears.

In the San Diego bus terminal she stood in front of a long line of pay phones, mesmerized by the way they caught the light, trying to remember a certain phone number and failing. She had a guidebook that was supposed to contain every youth hostel in the state of California, and the closest San Diego entry was miles from the bus terminal but she walked there anyway; a long walk down wide streets in the early evening, pavement still radiating heat from the afternoon sunlight, dance music pounding from slow-moving cars with tinted windows. Her suitcase made her a stranger, so she dropped it into a garbage can as she passed and after that she went on feeling light and infinitely anonymous, much less wary, much less sharp, hands in her pockets and sometimes whistling brief picked-up snatches of tunes that came and went. She passed a gospel church and sat for a while on the steps in the vertiginous twilight, the church and her soul both swelling with music, and then onward past a bodega where two small boys lingered in the doorway. They watched her and one said something in Spanish as she passed. She spoke to him in his own language and he smiled, abruptly shy, and she continued on in the last light of day. In those days she kept the lists in her pocket (languages, names), and it was excellent, the way the folded wads of paper fitted perfectly in her right hand.

On her first day in Rome she went to an internet café, and after some time she emerged with a phone number for a house in Quebec. In the motel room she sat for a long time holding the scrap of paper in her hands and then placed a wildly expensive long-distance call. A man answered on the second ring.

"Simon," she said.

"Who is this?" he asked, in French.

"*C'est moi.*"

"Lilia?"

"I just wanted to thank you," Lilia said.

Simon was quiet for a moment before he spoke. "Don't thank me," he said finally. "It was all I could do."

After an hour of conversation, she hung up the phone and went out into the city. She made her way back to the Tiber River and walked back to the same bridge, the lists far downstream and the policeman long departed, and stayed there for a long time looking down at the water. Ten years later she stood in the same place with her Italian husband on the day of their seventh anniversary of marriage, and he laughed when she imitated the policeman.

"It was scary," she insisted. "I thought I'd be arrested for littering and deported on the spot."

"I know," he said, still laughing. "You tell me that every year, my love, but when in your life were you ever scared?"

Once on a highway in the American mountains, once on a subway platform in Montreal. Seldom, in other words, but she was left with strange memories. It wasn't a question of unhappiness, but her thoughts drifted back at odd moments. When she was walking alone on certain boulevards in the rain: "There's a Central Australian language," Eli once told her, "that has a word, *nyimpe*, I'm mispronouncing it, that means 'the smell of rain.'" (Difficult now to remember his face. His hair was dark, but were his eyes brown or blue?) Or sometimes when she woke up in winter and the covers had fallen off the bed, the mere sensation of cold was enough to bring the streets of Montreal back to her; wandering with Michaela through the ice-locked landscape, arguing, shivering, talking in circles about memory and accidents. Michaela wasn't someone Lilia ever trusted, but there was a certain kinship. They shared a suspicion that the world might prove, in the end, to have been either a mirage or a particularly elaborate hoax.

Or when she stood in a metro station at the end of the day, waiting for the train that brought her from a translation job at the Vatican to the apartment she shared with her husband a few stops down the line, Lilia was sometimes shocked by a memory so forceful that it rendered her breathless. She could close her eyes and watch Michaela coming down the stairs at Métro Place-des-Arts. Michaela had been crying a short time earlier but she was smiling when she came to Lilia, a red cigarette box crushed in one hand. The moment Lilia saw her she stood up from the bench and started to repeat herself, *Tell me what happened*, but Michaela was smiling as she came toward her and she kissed Lilia lightly on the lips before Lilia could finish the sentence. Her lips were cold from the air aboveground.

"Listen," Michaela said. She put her hands on Lilia's shoulders then and whispered a story in her ear. It was an old story about broken windows and snow, over in a few sentences, and when she was done Lilia sank down onto the bench, staring up at her, shocked into silence. In a few minutes Eli would run past her screaming Michaela's name, in a few minutes the night would implode into noise and catastrophe, but for now Michaela stood near, watching her, and Lilia had never seen her so still or so calm. Michaela's voice was gentle when she spoke.

"Do you remember now?"

Lilia nodded. *Yes. I remember everything.*

"I've made my decision," Michaela said. Lilia was struck by a look she'd never seen before. There were tears in Michaela's eyes, but her face was radiant. "I'm leaving tonight."

Lilia swallowed and found her voice. "You sound happy."

"I am."

"Where are you going?"

"Far away," Michaela said. She smiled then, already leaving, and walked away down the platform to meet her train.

picador.com

blog
videos
interviews
extracts